Mills & Boon
Best Seller Romance

A chance to read and collect some of the best-loved novels from Mills & Boon—the world's largest publisher of romantic fiction.

Every month, four titles by favourite Mills & Boon authors will be re-published in the *Best Seller Romance* series.

A list of other titles in the *Best Seller Romance* series can be found at the end of this book.

Rebecca Stratton

THE WARM WIND OF FARIK

MILLS & BOON LIMITED
LONDON · TORONTO

First published 1975
Australian copyright 1981
Philippine copyright 1981
This edition 1981

© Rebecca Stratton 1975

ISBN 0 263 73593 1

Set in Linotype Times 11 on 12pt.

Made and printed in Great Britain by Richard Clay (The Chaucer Press) Ltd, Bungay, Suffolk

CHAPTER ONE

LINSIE PALMER had doubts. She had quite a number of doubts, mostly about letting Kadri drive the rather ramshackle car they had hired from their very friendly landlord at the hotel. Kadri Lemiz, with the fatalistic outlook of most Turks behind the wheel of a motor vehicle, seemed bent not only on self-destruction but on taking her with him, and she clung to the sides of the old vehicle with nervous fingers.

It was hot, hotter than anything she had ever known before, and the only consolation their speed offered was that it created a warm, light wind that did something towards cooling her. The lovely bay of Antalya looked like pure turquoise blue silk under the hot sky and across the other side of it the Bey Mountains rose majestically, shrouded in a heat haze that gave them a beautifully dreamy look.

As much as she had seen of Turkey before coming upon Antalya had been impressive enough, but nothing had prepared her for the beauty and sheer glorious lushness of the landscape here. Apart from the incredible turquoise colour of the Mediterranean at this point, there were the bright, multi-coloured rocks down which waterfalls cascaded from sheer cliffs into the sea.

There were acres of citrus groves, sweet-smelling and colourful, and thick, shady pine forests with the warm air constantly filled with the soft, cooling sound of running water. Present worries apart, Linsie felt, she could quite happily have spent the rest of her life there.

Even Kadri, who had spent holidays there before from his native Istanbul, found time to look around him and smile with pleasure at the magnificence of everything, even though every small distraction made Linsie cling more tightly to the edge of the car door.

She would far rather have driven the car herself, but for a Turkish man to allow a woman to drive him was unthinkable, so she had not pressed the point. She was glad enough to have him with her, for on her own she would have been regarded with the utmost suspicion in this country where women were still expected to behave with more reticence.

She had been fortunate in that Selim Alkilic, the proprietor of their hotel, was one of the more progressive men of his race. Having a daughter who was a practising doctor in one of the big city hospitals, and of whom he was very proud, had made him much more broad-minded and he had not refused outright to find Linsie a room, as many would have done with a young woman travelling alone. Kadri had joined her a couple of days later, and that, she thought, Selim Bey had viewed with rather more suspicion than her single state.

By the time Kadri arrived in Antalya she had already discovered that Celik Demaril lived in an almost inaccessible fortress of a place in the hills, called Farik. It was just outside the town, she had been told, though reluctantly, but its master was virtually un-

6

approachable and he would certainly not see a young, unaccompanied European woman like herself.

All this Selim Bey had told her with much earnestness and by way of a warning, she thought—for her own good. He was strangely unwilling to talk about either Farik or its owner, but Linsie was unsure whether ignorance of the man or caution was the reason. With Kadri as a companion she stood no more chance, he assured her solemnly, but—he shrugged with characteristic resignation—they could try, of course.

It was so desperately important to Linsie, this meeting with Celik Demaril, that she was prepared to go to almost any lengths to achieve it. For months she had plagued her father to let her take the assignment, although she had had little or no experience in field journalism and some of the staff of the magazine had gone so far as to suggest that she had been given such a plum assignment only because her father owned the magazine.

She had ignored the suggestions and assured her father that, given the chance, she had the makings of a good journalist, but to prove it she had to get in to see Celik Demaril or no one would believe her again, even her father.

It had been Kadri's father, an old friend of her own father's, weighing in with the assurance that he and his family would see that she came to no harm while she was in Turkey, who had tipped the balance. Linsie had a strong suspicion that he had foreseen many more problems for her than she had so far

7

encountered as a woman alone in Turkey, and that was the reason for his apparently being on her side, but she was too glad to have his support to look for reasons.

Kadri was a photographer of some note in his own right and he was to take the pictures to accompany her written feature about Celik Demaril—one of a series about eligible millionaires. So far, she had to admit, she had not been noticeably successful in getting to see him. Three times since her arrival she had tried to telephone the big white house on the hill and make an appointment to see the elusive millionaire, but each time her request for the number had been refused by the operator.

It was frustrating, but Linsie was far from ready to admit herself beaten, and this morning she intended trying the personal approach, despite Kadri's rather dubious reception of the idea. She had been prepared to come alone, but he would not hear of that, so here they both were speeding along the hilly road out of Antalya at a speed that took her breath away, considering the state of the road and the drop towards the sea on one side.

Kadri was good-looking in the deep, dark way of Turkish men, black-haired and brown-skinned with eyes almost as black as his hair, and warm and expressive as dark mirrors. He made no pretence of being unappreciative of her as a woman, although his manner towards her was at all times strictly polite, almost formal, despite the fact that they had met several times before in London.

8

Every so often his expressive brows rose and his eyes flickered briefly over her face while he smiled as if he was both appreciative of her looks but also amused by her obvious nervousness. And the latter she was bound to take exception to, sooner or later.

'I'm glad you find it funny,' she told him at last, her mouth reproachful, and Kadri laughed softly.

'I am not amused by you, Linsie,' he told her. 'I swear I am not!'

'You're amused because you know you're scaring the life out of me by driving like a madman,' Linsie retorted. 'Must you take this awful road at a hundred miles an hour, Kadri?'

'No more than fifty,' Kadri promised solemnly. 'Do you not trust me?'

'I'd rather have driven myself along these roads,' Linsie confessed, and he frowned in mild dislike.

'That is not possible, Linsie,' he said. 'Am I a man that I would trust my life to the driving of a woman?'

'I don't see why not,' Linsie told him reasonably. 'I'm trusting my life to you!'

Kadri sighed deeply but not, she suspected, sincerely, and he lifted one hand from the wheel and waved it expressively in the air by way of an answer. 'I think we are wasting our time by coming up here,' he told her, changing the subject, and Linsie looked at him curiously.

'You've said that before,' she reminded him. 'But it means a lot to me to get this interview, Kadri, and I mean to get in to see Celik Demaril somehow or other.'

Kadri shrugged and again, briefly, swept his dark, appreciative eyes over her as he smiled. 'If anyone can succeed, you can,' he said softly.

At twenty-two Linsie looked several years younger and found it not always an advantage. A pale, soft skin gave her a deceptively fragile look that was belied by a dogged determination whenever she had set her heart on anything, like this interview with the elusive millionaire.

Her hair was already very fair and would become even lighter after a few weeks in the sun, and it was soft, silky and thicker than fair hair often is. It complemented her deep blue eyes and was shades lighter than her naturaly darker brown lashes.

A pale blue cotton dress, sensibly sleeved against the sun that was hot even this early in the year, gave her an essentially English look and a small-brimmed denim hat that well matched her dress shaded her head and lent an extra blueness to her eyes. Her mouth curved softly in appreciation of the compliment, but she distorted it almost at once in a grimace, disliking the idea of being admitted only because she was a presentable-looking woman.

'I wish we knew a bit more about this Celik Demaril,' she said. 'We've heard so little about him, and either Selim Bey doesn't know anything or he isn't telling, for some reason best known to himself.'

Kadri was smiling in a rather annoyingly knowing way. 'Selim Bey probably knows which side his bread is buttered,' he told her, displaying a surprising knowledge of English slang. 'A man with as much

10

money as Celik Bey is bound to be influential, and Selim is a businessman!'

'You're probably right,' Linsie agreed. 'But that makes it all the more imperative that I see the man personally. There's no other way of writing the feature except by talking to him, and he seems very elusive so far.'

'We know that he is Italian from his mother's side,' Kadri recapped as they drove along the last mile towards the big house. 'And we know that he likes to sail.'

'Do we?' Linsie looked at him curiously, her blue eyes narrowed thoughtfully. 'You kept that bit of information quiet.'

Kadri shrugged. 'I thought everyone knew—he keeps his yacht in the bay.'

'Does he?' She hastily went over in her mind all the boats she had seen moored in the harbour at Antalya, and eventually recalled a huge white, gleaming craft that was virtually impossible to overlook. How she could have forgotten it, she had no idea, but she nodded when she remembered. 'That might be useful,' she remarked, and Kadri looked at her briefly over one shoulder.

'I do not quite see how,' he said.

Linsie shrugged, not quite sure herself yet, what use the information could be, but it was useful to have any morsel of knowledge about her quarry. If Celik Demaril liked to sail and he sailed from Antalya, as presumably he did if his boat was kept there, then it could be useful one day.

'It might be,' she assured Kadri. 'I could always stow away if it came to the pinch.'

Kadri almost swerved them off the road in his alarm, and he sent another, frankly stunned, look over his shoulder. 'You would surely not do such a thing?' he said.

'I surely would,' Linsie vowed, quite intrigued with the idea in its present, rather vague form. 'I hope it won't be necessary to resort to anything like that, but if there was no other way of getting to him, then I would.'

Kadri looked very Turkish and very disapproving as he frowned over her determination. 'It would not be—seemly,' he decreed solemnly, and Linsie was so surprised at the old-fashioned phrase that for a moment she stared at him without answering. No matter how progressive the Turkish male might be outwardly, there were always limits to his broadmindedness.

'It's important to me to get to see Celik Demaril,' she pointed out yet again. 'How I do it depends on how far I have to go to achieve my object. I don't relish stowing away on the wretched man's yacht, but if I have to I will, Kadri, make no mistake about that!'

'I cannot think,' Kadri stated firmly, 'that Stephen Bey, your father, means you to go to those lengths!'

'He want a story, an interview with Celik Demaril,' Linsie insisted. 'I'm a reporter and he expects me to use the same methods his other people would.'

'Not something so unwomanly,' Kadri argued adamantly. 'And I cannot allow you to do such a thing, Linsie. Not while you are in my care.'

Linsie looked at him for a moment, a little startled by his statement that she was in his care. Certainly his father had assured her own less apprehensive parent that he and his family would take care of her, but she had taken the promise at face value. That Kadri would take it to mean that she was under his protection, literally, in the way one of the women-folk of his own family would be, had never even occurred to her.

'The fact that you promised to take care of me doesn't mean you have to dog my footsteps, you know,' she told him, glancing from the corner of her eye to see how he was taking it. 'I'm quite capable of taking care of myself, and Pop would expect me to. As for not allowing me to——' She shook her head and smiled knowingly. 'You're not my keeper, Kadri, and you don't have the last word on what I do.'

'I see!' His good-looking face had a tight closed look suddenly and she realised that she had been too blunt, gone too far in asserting her right to be com-pletely independent. Kadri would not understand either her wish to be independent or her refusal to be coddled in a way that his own womenfolk would take for granted.

She wished she had been less outspoken, less wounding to his male pride and impulsively, as she did so many things, she put a hand on his arm, feeling the tightly tensed muscles under his shirt sleeve. 'I'm sorry, Kadri,' she said softly. 'I didn't mean that to sound quite the way it did. Will you forgive me?'

He turned his head briefly and looked at her over his shoulder, and she used her eyes without shame to add to her plea for forgiveness. 'Of course,' he said quietly, and a small, rueful smile tugged at his mouth as he took another sharp bend. 'I must get used to your independence, Linsie. I am not accustomed to your ways and sometimes I am shocked like—a little old lady?'

Linsie laughed, and squeezed the arm she still held, her eyes bright with relief that he was so willing to be mollified. She would hate to lose Kadri's support, and if she was completely honest she was glad not to have to tackle the problem of approaching Celik Demaril without his aid.

'I shock my own grandmother sometimes,' she admitted. 'I shouldn't let my enthusiasm run away with me, but I sometimes speak and act first and think afterwards—when it's too late.'

Kadri looked dubious. 'I hope you will not act too impulsively in this present situation,' he warned her. 'You could be more sorry than even you can imagine.'

She said nothing in reply, for they were already at the tall and rather formidable gates of Farik, the big white house in the hills, and her heart was racing wildly, partly in excitement and partly in apprehension, although she refused to recognise the latter.

It was large and white and the roof was almost flat, with red tiles and eaves that overhung the balconied windows jutting above the enclosed garden. A metal-studded door was closed against any sort of intrusion even if one could obtain admission to the walled garden, and that seemed unlikely in view of the tall, wrought iron gates that were locked when Linsie tried them.

Tall slim cypresses stood like dark sentinels before the house and a riot of every kind of tree and flowering shrub gave colour and scent to as tranquil a scene as she had ever seen. Creamy magnolias and the pink blossom of tamarisk contrasted palely with the darkness of the cypresses, and a huge bougainvillea wound its way round every shuttered window, set open to the light warm wind off the sea.

It was so much more beautiful than she had expected that for a moment she did no more than stand and wonder, her purpose momentarily forgotten. Kadri, less keen on the expedition, stayed in the car for a moment, watching her with anxious eyes through the windscreen.

It was just as she was about to look for some means of summoning a porter or someone that a short, stout man appeared as if from nowhere and regarded her through the ornate bars of the gate with bright, dark, suspicious eyes.

He spoke to her in Turkish which she made no pretence of understanding, but looked back at Kadri for a translation. 'He says that there is no admission to strangers,' Kadri informed her. 'And will the lady please to go away.'

'Tell him,' Linsie insisted, still with one hand firmly round the resistant bars, 'that I am from England and that I wish to see Mr. Demaril on very important business.'

'But, Linsie, that is not true,' Kadri denied with a worried frown. 'I cannot tell him——'

'Tell him,' Linsie urged. 'I'll take the blame if anything happens.'

Unhappy about the whole thing, Kadri presumably did as she said, although she had no way of knowing how faithfuly he had translated her words. Whatever he said, it was obvious that it made no difference at all to the old man's determination to keep them out. His grizzled head in its small round cap shook adamantly, and he waved a hand in such a way that it was obvious what his answer was even before Kadri translated it.

'It is no use, Linsie,' Kadri told her. 'He will not open the gate, and he says no one can see Celik Bey without an appointment.'

'Then make an appointment,' Linsie told him swiftly. 'Tell him I must see Mr. Demaril and I want to make an appointment.'

His sigh was as much resigned as unwilling, but he apparently did as she asked, and the old man behind the gates looked at her for a moment curiously. When he spoke again it was obvious that he was asking a question and she saw the faint hint of a smile on Kadri's mouth as he shrugged in that expressive and telling way that all his race did.

He said something more to the old man and he nodded, then waved his hands again as he spoke, turning his back on them after a moment and walking away. 'Has he gone to ask if he'll see us?' she asked

Kadri hopefully, and he shook his head.

'I doubt it,' he told her. 'He says it is as well to humour foreign ladies when they have crazy ideas, but he has not much hope that Celik Bey will even consider such an interview.'

'You told him I was a journalist?' she asked, not at all sure that that had been a good idea, and Kadri nodded.

'I thought I might as well,' he said. 'Hence his opinion of you as a crazy foreign lady.'

'I see!' Linsie's blue eyes sparkled determinedly. 'Well, if you've scuttled my chances of an interview, Kadri Lemiz, I'll sack you on the spot and carry on this assignment on my own!'

He was already shaking his head, a hint of smile again on his face. 'I do not think that would be wise, Linsie Hanim,' he told her softly. 'I think there will come a time when you will need me. Turkish men do not like to be so relentlessly pursued, and Celik Demaril is a very powerful man, he might——' His shrug was expressive and for some reason it sent a small warning shiver along her spine.

Glancing along the shrub-lined path that led to the big metal-studded doors of the house, Linsie bit her lip, a doubt entering her head for the first time. 'I—I don't see what he can do,' she said with admirable bravado. 'But maybe you're right about staying with me. I wish I could speak at least some Turkish—I've only just realised that this wretched man probably doesn't speak any English.'

She could not imagine why Kadri looked suddenly

rather sick, but she had her answer a second later when a voice spoke from behind the still closed gates and startled her so much that she made an audible sound of surprise.

'That is your second mistake, *hanim*,' the quiet voice informed her in excellent English. 'The first was in coming to my gate and demanding admittance on a false claim of important business.'

Linsie stared for a moment, unable to believe that it had been so easy, for this must surely be Celik Demaril himself, and he was quite a surprise in himself. She had expected someone as least as dark as Kadri, but this man was much fairer, at least as far as his hair was concerned.

Instead of being black, as she had expected, his was no more than dark brown, although his skin was a dark golden brown which made his eyes even more startling. They were not the dark, luminous orbs she expected but a bright, startling blue.

He was tall and there was no sign of superfluous flesh anywhere on that long body, and he looked powerful, perhaps, she considered with a slight shiver, slightly dangerous if he was roused to anger. He wore European dress, as Kadri did, and this was some consolation to her in some odd way, but for all that he looked much more eastern than European.

A lightweight suit in cream was expensively tailored to fit the lean body to perfection and a brown shirt exposed several inches of strong brown throat and neck. Altogether, she thought slightly dizzily, he was quite unexpected and much more attractive than she could have anticipated.

'I'm sorry to have disturbed you,' she managed at last in a slightly shaky voice. 'I—I presume you are Mr. Demaril?' she ventured as an afterthought, and she saw the thin mouth twitch briefly in what could as easily have been a sneer or a smile.

'I happened to be close at hand when you made that incredible statement to my servant about having important business with me,' he told her, and it was obvious from the way he spoke that he considered she had taken a quite unforgivable liberty. 'I have to inform you, *hanim*,' he went on before she could say another word in her own defence, 'that I do not make appointments at my garden gate, and certainly not with young women I have never seen in my life before, nor have the slightest wish to see again. You will do me the favour, *hanim*, of leaving my premises and not returning.'

Without more ado he turned on his heel and strode back along the path to the house, his back tall and straight, and leaving Linsie staring after him with her mouth slightly open and her hands clenched tightly round the bars of the gate.

It was Kadri's voice that recalled her, and by that time her quarry had disappeared into the scented vegetation that surrounded his home. 'Linsie?' He leaned out of the window and frowned at her. 'Are you coming back?'

For a moment she did not move, then she turned and looked at him with a bright glint of determination in her blue eyes 'This time he gets away with it,' she said. 'Next time I'll be more cunning!' She turned again briefly and looked at the big white house and the tranquil beauty of its setting.

'I haven't finished with Mr. Celik Demaril by a long way yet!'

CHAPTER TWO

'It could work,' Linsie insisted, knowing how much Kadri would dislike the idea.

It was two whole days now since she had been so summarily dismissed by Celik Demaril and turned away from the gates of Farik, and she was determined to find some other method of approaching him. She was convinced that once he realised how much the interview meant to her he would consent to see her, and even let Kadri take his pictures, although that part of it could be dispensed with if it was absolutely out of the question.

It was through her efforts that she had discovered the fact that every week three women from a nearby village went up to the house on the hill with laundry. It had taken her only a few seconds to see this simple weekly episode as a way of solving her own predicament.

The women took a couple of donkeys with them

and carried the washing in large baskets balanced either side of the patient little animals. It was a long and inevitably tiring climb and she would probably suffer terribly from the heat, but it was so far the best way yet that had presented itself and she was determined to try it.

Kadri was not in favour, but that was no more than she had expected and she refused to admit defeat until it was staring her in the face. Surely no man could be as autocratically uncaring as Celik Demaril had given the impression of being and once she could get near enough to talk to him without that restricting gate between them, he would almost certainly see reason, she felt sure.

'I wish you would not be so—so persistent,' Kadri told her, a little disturbed by her, as he saw it, unfeminine determination. 'It is not expected of a young woman to insist on meeting a man against his will,' he went on. 'You must realise that, Linsie.'

'I do realise it—from your point of view, and perhaps from his,' she admitted. 'But looking at it from my angle, my father, and the editor of *Woman of Taste* in particular, will expect me to produce an article about Celik Demaril and they won't care much how I get it.'

'But they will surely not expect you to—to cheapen yourself by actually chasing the man,' Kadri said, mildly scandalised, and Linsie smiled at him ruefully.

Pushing back the long hair from her forehead, she looked at him with challenging eyes. 'Is that how you see me?' she asked.

He shook his head swiftly to deny it. 'No, no, of course not,' he assured her. 'But I am thinking of the impression you will give Celik Bey if you do as you now propose to do.'

Linsie's eyes sparkled with enthusiasm for her scheme and she was in no mood to be deterred. 'I think it's a foolproof scheme,' she told him defiantly. 'And I'm sure it'll work.'

'As sure as I am that such a man would never come into contact with his laundrywomen,' he told her wryly. 'It has no chance of succeeding and you will be forcibly ejected from the place like a—like a common criminal, especially since I cannot be there to plead for you.'

'Like suggesting that I'm a slightly cuckoo foreign lady, like you did last time?' Linsie suggested.

'By explaining your reasons,' Kadri said, trying not to sound as if he also disapproved of such unladylike language.

'I can do that myself once I get past those gates,' Linsie assured him with a confident smile. 'It's just that first step inside that I need, and this idea will take care of that.'

He still looked dubious, no matter how much she reassured him, and he shook his head in despair. 'You realise that you will have to walk all the way up there?' he said, and she nodded. 'You could not do it, Linsie.'

'Yes, I could,' she argued, and her father would have recognised the glint in her eyes and yielded at that point. 'I know I'll probably get hot and tired, but if the other women can do it then so can I.'

'But they are accustomed to doing the same journey every week,' Kadri pointed out reasonably. 'You are not—you will faint, or collapse with fatigue and the whole thing will have been a waste of time.'

'Not if I put my mind to it,' she insisted, refusing to see anything but the future success of her interview as the outcome of her scheme. 'I'll go in with them and then go in search of Celik Demaril and let him know who I am and why I'm there. I've watched them and seen how they walk with their heads down whenever a man comes near them—I can do the same and no one will know any different.'

'But you cannot——'

'The next time they go up there, I'll be with them!' Linsie insisted, refusing to listen to his argument.

Kadri looked at her for a moment and she could guess that he was having to see a certain crazy logic in her plan, but he would be reluctant to admit it, and instead continue to oppose her. 'And which of the women do you imagine is going to allow you to take her place?' he asked.

Linsie shrugged, not having yet sorted out the finer points of her plan. 'Oh, one of them will,' she said confidently. 'I can make it worth her while, whichever one it is. Maybe Selim Bey would know which one of them would be most willing to help.'

Kadri's dark eyes rolled heavenwards in appeal and he spread his hands. 'Not Selim Bey,' he begged. 'Do not involve any more people in your scheme, I beg you, Linsie Hanim. It is possible that Selim would think it his duty to inform the man of your scheme, and then——' He spread his hands in a gesture that was both appeal and resignation. 'Who knows what such a man would do?'

'You think Selim would tell him?' Linsie looked dubious for a moment, obliged to face the first snag, but then she shrugged. 'Oh well, perhaps you're right about him—I'll decide myself which one of the women to ask.'

'If only you would not——' Kadri began, but a swift and haughty toss of her head silenced him and he resigned himself to the inevitable with another shrug of his expressive shoulders.

'I shall need to borrow some of her clothes too,' Linsie mused, then suddenly noticed his gloomy face and shook her head. 'Oh, come on, cheer up,' she admonished him. 'I'm hungry, how about treating me to a good solid meal, just in case I get thrown into jail and get nothing but bread and water for a month —or whatever it is you feed your Turkish prisoners with.'

She was laughing at the idea of going to jail, but Kadri looked as if he thought the prospect more than likely, and wondered how he was ever going to explain such a thing to her father. For herself, Linsie did not even consider it failing, and she ate a huge meal of *döner kebab* with no other thought in her mind than enjoying the delicious spit-roasted lamb with pilaf rice. Kadri, she failed to notice, ate much less and seemed rather preoccupied.

It was not as easy as Linsie had anticipated, persuading one of the laundrywomen to let her take her place, and for a moment she wondered if Kadri had said more in his translation of her request than she meant him to.

Eventually, however, the youngest of the three, less inhibited than her older companions and with a husband who was more progressive in his outlook, agreed to let Linsie take her place and also to borrow some of her clothes.

She seemed to consider the whole thing as a huge joke, and indulged in a great deal of giggling and collapsing in fits of laughter at the prospect of the English *hanim* wearing her clothes in public. She helped Linsie to dress in the voluminous white trousers which she refered to as *salver* and which completely disguised any shape she had.

A white embroidered blouse followed, then a striped one, and a wrap-around skirt of some coarse brown material; the blouses were topped by an embroidered jacket, pretty enough to bring favourable comment from Linsie, and her benefactor insisted on a necklace of blue beads which, she informed her via Kadri, would ward off the evil eye.

The whole costume was topped by the indispensable headcloth that was to be her main disguise, and her co-conspirator arranged it very carefully so as to exclude all sight of her bright fair hair. Having fixed it to her satisfaction she then instructed Linsie, by way of hand signs, how to tuck it across the lower part of her face as a veil. Standing back to admire her handiwork, she seemed pleased that Linsie was satisfied, and they went out to show Kadri the finished effect.

The woman said a word or two to Kadri and giggled uncontrollably, her bright dark eyes shining with mischief as she visualised the consternation of the *Aga* when he was confronted with such an unusual washerwoman.

'You do actually see him, don't you?' Linsie asked, anxious to have the fact confirmed, especially in view of Kadri's earlier doubts. His translation, however, brought a shake of her head, and Linsie bit her lip at the prospect of a setback. 'Oh well, then I'll just have to go and look for him,' she declared, but sounded a little less confident, a fact that Kadri noted with narrowed eyes.

'You knew you would not find it easy, Linsie,' Kadri told her, still anxious for her to change her mind. 'I told you that such a man as Celik Demaril would not have contact with washerwomen.' He looked at her for a moment, then shook his head. 'Not that you will go long undetected,' he assured her.

'Oh, stop being such a wet blanket!' she told him with an edge of impatience on her voice, caused by a new uncertainty, and he looked at her curiously for a moment, trying to find sense in the unfamiliar phrase.

'A wet blanket?' he enquired politely, and she shrugged.

'Oh, it's just a saying,' she told him. 'It means you're trying to discourage me instead of lending your support, and I wish you wouldn't.'

'Because I cannot agree with such a mad scheme,' Kadri insisted quietly. 'I wish you would have another thought about it, Linsie, before it is too late.'

'It's already too late,' she retorted, looking down at the shape-concealing costume and experiencing her first taste of nerves when she thought of passing through those formidable gates in disguise. 'Nermin's gone to a lot of trouble dressing me in this lot,' she told him, determinedly dismissing her own traitorous doubts. 'I don't propose going back on it now!'

Kadri looked more or less resigned, but he still had one more try. 'And you mean to walk all the way up there?' he asked.

'Of course!'

'Are you not very hot?' he insisted, and she looked at the watching Nermin with some envy.

The Turkish girl appeared unbelievably cool in her collection of garments as heavy as Linsie's, but already her own body was feeling the effects of carrying so much unaccustomed weight, and she had yet to climb the steep, rough hill in the heat of the sun.

'I'll cope,' she told him shortly, and smiled at the girl, then pulled a face. 'How do you cope with the heat?' she asked, and when Kadri translated her question, Nermin looked puzzled.

'Did I not say it was a matter of custom?' Kadri asked with forgivable smugness. 'The woman is used to such garments, you are not, Linsie, and you would be wiser to admit that you are wrong and change your mind.'

27

'I'll do no such thing,' Linsie declared, her chin stuck out so that the headcloth slipped a little and she made a wild grab at it, her fair skin and bright blue eyes plainly visible.

'Then in the name of mercy keep your head down,' Kadri begged. 'For no one will admit a fair and blue-eyed Turk to the house of Celik Demaril!'

Reminded of something, Linsie frowned for a moment. 'That was strange,' she mused, momentarily distracted from her main purpose. 'You probably didn't see from the car, but he has blue eyes.'

Kadri looked at her for a moment almost as if he didn't believe her, then he shrugged. 'He is not wholly Turkish,' he reminded her. 'That could account for it.'

'The other half is Italian, if our information's right,' she said. 'And they're almost as dark as Turks as a rule.' She tapped one thumbnail against her teeth for a moment thoughtfully. 'Oh well,' she said at last, 'that's just one more mystery to be solved when I finally get to grips with the mysterious Celik Bey.'

Linsie set one foot in front of the other almost mechanically trying to keep pace with her companions, but their steady, plodding pace was proving too much for her and she licked her dry lips as she held on to the basket of clean laundry hung from the donkey's back.

Even with the assistance of that patient little beast she was almost at the end of her endurance, and her body felt so hot and uncomfortable that she could have stripped off every stitch there and then and revelled in the touch of the warm wind on her skin. Even pouring rain would have been welcome as long as it cleansed her skin of that insufferable heat.

Bedia, the older of the two women, turned her head once or twice and looked at her enquiringly, but so far Linsie had managed to smile reassuringly and the woman had returned to her almost silent plodding up the hill. Now that they were almost within sight of the gates of Farik, Linsie had no intention of giving up, not with her goal in sight.

Another few yards and they turned off along the outer wall of the garden, taking the back way in, of course—she should have realised that. Bedia and the other woman led the donkeys, although the animals had done the journey so often that they could probably have come alone.

Huge plane trees cast welcome shadow across their path and Linsie chanced a moment or two with her veil down so that she could enjoy at least a moment of the cool. The light green leaves stirred softly over their heads and she thought longingly of cool drinks and iced melon. Not that she had even the remotest chance of being treated like a visitor, even when it was discovered who she was, but it gave her a moment of pleasure to simply think about it.

Bedia said something to her in Turkish and she was obliged to shrug helplessly, at which Bedia shook her head in regret. They went in through a smaller, less impressive gate than the ones she had seen before, but they were admitted by the same short, stout man she had seen then and she hastily lowered her eyes and put a hand to make sure her veil was in place as she walked past him.

The rear of the house was only slightly less impressive than the front, and the old man had now been joined by a young boy and two other women, so that there was much talk now from her two companions as they exchanged greetings. It seemed as if they were trying to cover up her own silence, but their efforts looked likely to prove in vain, for after several curious looks in her direction, the old man spoke to her directly.

Linsie shook her head and Bedia at once said something to him, shaking her own head and making regretful noises, so that Linsie wondered what on earth she could have been telling him was the reason for her own silence. It was enough that the man was satisfied for the moment and she heaved a great sigh of relief when he turned and resumed his conversation with the others.

It was while the others were unloading the laundry baskets that she decided to slip away, hoping to be unseen, for if she was seen and stopped by one of the servants the whole gruelling experience could have been in vain, for they would make sure she never got within speaking distance of their employer.

She caught Bedia's rather anxious eyes on her as she slipped away round the side of the house and in a moment she was safely hidden in a mass of flowering shrubs, her breath coming short and harsh in her throat as she made no attempt to walk in the slow plod she had used as a disguise, but sped as fast as she could.

Suddenly less tired now that excitement was taking over, she stood for a moment to get her bearings and to try and decide just where she could look for the man she had taken so much trouble to try and see. It was cool under the shade of the shrubs and trees and she took a while to breathe the scented air that seemed to flow round her like a scent-laden cloud.

Her eyes half closed in the sheer bliss of it, she opened them wide a second later and gave a small cry of alarm when a voice spoke behind her. *'Bir dakika!'* the voice commanded sternly in incomprehensible Turkish. *'Ne istiyorsunuz?'*

Linsie's first instinct was to flee. If some officious servant stopped her now, she was lost, but even as she toyed with the idea of running a large hand fastened itself round her upper arm and swung her round and she realised without looking up that it was no servant who had her captive but Celik Damaril himself.

Now that she was faced with him she felt dismayingly uncertain of herself and of her right to be there in the circumstances, and without waiting to reason she snatched her arm from his hold and ran, sparing a moment to pull the concealing veil across her face more firmly.

Running was not easy in the voluminous costume she was wearing and she stumbled as she turned the corner of the house and almost fell, colliding at the same time with someone coming from the opposite

31

direction. Her legs as weak as water, she spared only a glance for the woman she had bumped into, then gasped an apology and would have run on.

There was a cry from behind her, again in Turkish, and the hand on her arm, so far gentle, tightened slightly and the woman looked at Celik Demaril curiously while doing as he had bade her do—namely hold Linsie and prevent her running away.

She was breathing heavily and her eyes were wide and half fearful above the concealing veil so that the woman who held on to her looked curiously at both her and her pursuer. He looked so fiercely stern as he came closer that her heart was hammering in her breast as if it would escape and her whole body was trembling.

The woman, she managed to note, was several inches taller than she was herself and had fair hair just turning grey, with bright blue eyes that looked somehow strangely familiar. She was smiling suddenly, and that Linsie found more encouraging.

The fair woman murmured some words softly in Turkish, and her voice was gently enquiring, but Celik Demaril made a short harsh sound that was suspiciously like a snort of disgust as he joined them. 'Do not waste time with Turkish, Mama,' he told the woman. 'This young woman is English!'

'So?' The gentle blue eyes looked at her with some surprise, as well they might, Linsie thought ruefully, for to all outward appearance she was a Turkish village woman.

Linsie found the scrutiny of two pairs of eyes not

only discomfiting but, in Celik Demaril's case, positively menacing. He seemed even taller at close quarters than he had behind those restraining gates the other day, and the dark, hawkish features were quite unrelenting as he gazed down at her with those oddly unfitting blue eyes.

He wore a suit very similar to the one he had worn the last time she saw him, only this one was pale fawn instead of cream and the shirt was white and therefore even more revealing as it contrasted with that strong brown neck and throat.

Obviously the woman was his mother, judging by the way he had addressed her, but again Linsie was puzzled, for this woman was almost as fair as she was herself, apart from a smooth golden skin that was enviably good for her age.

'So, you are here again, despite my warning!'

His voice broke harshly into her rather dazed musings and she attempted to pull the veil across her face, though she knew the attempt was useless. A large and not very gentle hand reached out and snatched the veil away and she felt herself shivering with apprehension. Never in her life had she felt so afraid of anyone and the feeling was not at all to her liking.

'White skin and blue eyes!' he jeered, as if such points were eminently undesirable. 'And you think to pass yourself off as a Turkish woman!'

She looked up at him at last and there was a hint of appeal in her blue eyes, but it went unheeded as far as her captor was concerned. His own gaze was hard and unrelenting.

33

'I—I want to explain,' she began, but with little hope of being allowed to do so. 'I had to see you to——'

'I made it plain that I did not wish to see you,' he interrupted harshly. 'I do not know your reason for making this unlawful entry into my home, but since you are a stranger in my country I will allow you to leave without making charges against you. But you will leave now!'

'Oh, but——' Linsie thought of the long, hot walk down the hill again without even a moment's respite before she started and she bit her lip. Also she was bitterly disappointed that what she had foreseen as an easy task once she had gained access to the house and gardens was proving nothing of the sort in actual fact. 'I'm—I'm terribly hot and tired,' she told him, hoping for a glimmer of compassion, although the blue eyes gave little hope of it. 'If I could——'

'If you are too hot then I suggest you dispense with at least some of that costume,' he said without offering any more agreeable solution, and it was the older woman who made a moue of reproach at him, not Linsie herself.

'Celik, *caro*,' she told him, 'you cannot send this poor young lady away with such little thought. Have you no compassion, *mio figlio*?'

It was plain that he did not like either the suggestion that he was acting harshly, or that he was unreasonable, but he shook his head firmly and his mouth was set firmly in a straight line, so that Linsie at least, had little hope of his changing his mind.

34

'I do not like being invaded in my own home, Mama,' he said firmly. 'You know that quite well.'

Despite the fact that she was feeling increasingly like weeping from sheer exhaustion and frustration, Linsie tried not to lose sight of her original objective, and she tried again to explain. 'I'm—I'm a journalist, Mr. Demaril,' she told him, licking her lips anxiously for fear he gave her no more time to have her say. 'I—I have to see you and talk to you about——'

He glared down at her with hard, glittering blue eyes and his mouth was almost cruel in its tightness. 'I never talk to journalists,' he informed her bluntly. 'And never to unaccompanied young women!'

He was, in Linsie's opinion, simply being stubborn and very Turkish with his jibe about unaccompanied young women, and she began to lose her temper. She stamped her foot, a gesture that startled him, she was satisfied to note, and he frowned the more, even though she suspected that the older woman found the exchange intriguing rather than distressing now that Linsie was showing signs of defending herself.

'You're biased and—and unreasonable!' she accused, uncaring if he took offence or not. 'All I wanted was a few minutes of your time—it means a lot to me!'

Swiftly, but with unmistakable meaning, the blue eyes swept over her from head to foot and once again that thin mouth was drawn into a hint of cruelty. 'You cannot afford my time,' he told her, his English more pedantic than ever, despite the words he chose. 'And I do not like being fooled by childish attempts at disguise—please leave my house at once!'

Again the older woman intervened, a reproachful look in her eyes, although Linsie suspected that she would limit her defiance of him. 'Celik!' she said softly, and he looked at her with cool, glittering eyes.

'Do not try and persuade me, Mama,' he told her sternly. 'You know my rules—I do not like to see them broken and I will not tolerate a journalist under my roof!'

When Linsie thought of all the agony she had suffered to get here, suffocated in that heavy costume, she could have wept in anger and frustration and she clenched her hands tightly, standing her ground despite the hint of threat in his last words.

'There's nothing childish about it!' she denied angrily. 'I had a job to do and I meant to do it!'

'So you bribed one of the laundrywomen to let you take her place,' he jeered, his gaze scornful. 'You must have thought me a fool to think I would not see through your—your disguise!' He reached out again and this time pulled the headcloth from her so roughly that her long fair hair fell about her face and shoulders. 'Your skin, your eyes, your hair, all of them the wrong colour—did you not realise how easily your attempts could be penetrated?'

'Of course I did!' she retorted, not without satisfaction. Shaking back her hair, she gave him a look from below her lashes, daring him to argue how successful her tactics had been in breaching his defences. 'I got this far—I got in to see you,' she reminded him.

'But you did not get what you wanted,' he argued,

and she could not resist a smile.

'You're talking to me,' she reminded him. 'That was the object of the whole thing.'

The tall sinewy body was drawn up sharply and for a moment she felt that stark flicker of fear again as she met the dark anger in those blue eyes. 'I do not like to be tricked,' he said in a cold, hard voice. 'You will leave now, *hanim*, or I will have my servants dispose of you!'

It was ridiculous, of course, to take such a threat literally, but there was something chillingly menacing about the way he said it that made her think he was quite capable of carrying out his threat. The older woman, she noticed, was looking as if she had resigned her attempts to influence him, and was shaking her head, a moue of regret pushing out her full lips as she looked at Linsie.

'Mr. Demaril——'

He said no more, but Linsie found herself taken firmly by one arm and forcibly dragged towards the wrought iron gates she had sought so hard to enter before. He held her tightly while he took a key from a jacket pocket and opened the gates.

'I will not say it again,' he informed her in a short, harsh voice. 'Go!'

'Wait!'

She staggered and almost fell as he pushed her through the gateway, then she ran back and clung to the iron bars as he locked the gate again. He did not even look at her but strode back the way he had come, and she was left clinging to the bars.

'My head,' she cried after him. 'I've nothing on my head—the sun, I can't——'

She saw the older woman bend and retrieve her headcloth where he had flung it down on to the ground, and he snatched it from her and strode back again, flinging the dusty headgear over the top of the gate without a word, and Linsie, for some reason, suddenly sat down under the shade of the plane trees and cried.

CHAPTER THREE

THE hardest part of all was telling Kadri that the mission had failed, just as he had foretold it would. At least it had failed to produce anything useful in the way of copy, which was the main object of it, and Linsie had endured all that heat and discomfort for virtually nothing. The only consolation was that she had managed to breach the apparently unsurmountable defences of the house on the hill. Linsie had met not only Celik Demaril but his mother too, and there, she thought, she had an ally, albeit a hesitant one.

Thinking about the fair-haired woman again she frowned curiously and wondered if it was possible that their information about Celik Demaril's parentage could have been wrong. True, the few words of endearment the woman had used were in what Linsie took for Italian, but she was not expert enough to be absolutely certain, and she would not have expected a native of Italy to be blonde and blue-eyed.

Kadri could offer no explanation, but he did seem quite relieved that she had returned from Farik unscathed, despite the fact that she had been more or less thrown out of the place by its owner. He probably expected her to give up the chase now and decide that Celik Demaril was an unattainable target for any journalist, let alone an inexperienced one like herself.

'What will you do now?' Kadri asked, as they sat eating dinner that night, and she knew exactly how his mind was working.

She shrugged, spearing an elusive piece of *baklava*, then lifting the syrup-soaked pastry to her lips with quite unladylike relish. 'Try again, of course,' she informed him as offhandedly as if it would be little trouble to do just that.

Kadri stared at her for a moment, his own appetite lessening suddenly at the prospect of there being another incident like today. 'I do not understand you, Linsie Hanim,' he said solemnly. 'You cannot mean that you mean to try and visit the house again. Such a thing would be madness, and I am sure that your father would not approve of such a thing.'

'He probably wouldn't,' Linsie agreed readily. 'But there are more ways of killing a cat, you know.'

She looked at him, her eyes bright and gleaming with determination, and Kadri looked completely confused as well as apprehensive. 'I do not understand this reference to a cat,' he told her, and she smiled, shaking her head, popping in the last few pistachio nuts and the last sweet threads of honey.

'It means,' she explained patiently, 'that there is more than one way of doing a thing. If one thing fails, one simply tries another, that's all.'

'Oh no!' Kadri appealed to Allah in a fervent little prayer and eyed her with plaintive appeal, his liquid dark eyes pleading with her not to indulge in any more escapades like that which had just failed so miserably. 'Please, Linsie,' he begged, 'will you not go home? Or else come back with me to Istanbul and enjoy a holiday with my family?'

'Behave like a lady, you mean?' Linsie suggested, her eyes taunting him for the suggestion. 'I don't give up that easily, Kadri, I thought you realised that!'

'If I had known you as well as I assumed I did,' Kadri assured her earnestly, 'I would not have attached myself to this assignment! I shall be prematurely in my grave, *hanim*, if you continue in this way!'

'Then go home!' Linsie told him, but hoped he wouldn't take her at her word. Knowing that Kadri was there in the background was definitely reassuring and she would hate it if he really did pack up and leave her.

'That I cannot do, as well you know!' He looked at her again with that appealing, earnest look that was so very hard to resist. 'Will you not, for my sake, take more care, Linsie? It would distress me terribly if something should happen to you, especially when my father has put you under my protection!'

'I'm quite capable to taking care of myself,' Linsie assured him, and was immediately sorry for having belittled his part in her well-being. She reached across and touched his hand lightly with her fingertips, a gesture he allowed with a certain hesitancy. 'I'm sorry, Kadri,' she said softly. 'I know you mean well, but I'm not in need of protection, not like your sisters. Leyla and Suna would expect you to take care of them, and they'd need you to, but I don't. I've travelled in other countries on my own and managed to survive.'

He took that information with a hint of doubt, one dark brow raised in question. 'I have heard only of you going to France alone,' he told her. 'Have you been elsewhere?'

'Well, no,' Linsie admitted reluctantly, wondering how he came to be so well informed unless her father had told him. 'I went there on my own for two weeks last year and I was perfectly all right.'

'Two weeks with a family in France is not the same as careering all over Turkey alone,' Kadri pointed out quietly, and again betraying an unexpected knowledge of her affairs. 'The Duboque family are friends of your father also, are they not?'

'They are.' She looked at him from below her lashes and then pulled a wry face. 'I suppose Pop's been telling tales out of school,' she guessed, and he smiled.

When Kadri smiled like that it was like a light in

those dark, luminous eyes and his teeth gleamed whitely in the handsome brown face. 'Stephen Bey told my father that you were unaccustomed to travelling abroad on your own, except for that one brief family holiday,' he informed her frankly. 'And my father and I promised that no harm would come to you.'

'Oh, I see!' She did not relish the idea of being looked upon as an innocent abroad, but she supposed her father had meant well, and he did worry about her, more than he admitted, since her mother died.

'It is natural that a father should be concerned about the safety of his only daughter,' Kadri told her, and she nodded, a little smile of admission acknowledging the fact.

'Yes, of course it is,' she said, and a second later laughed softly, then hastily smothered it when Kadri looked at her in astonishment. 'I was just thinking,' she told him, 'what Pop would have made of today's little adventure.'

'He would not have been happy, I think,' Kadri said seriously, and Linsie thought he was probably right.

It was while she was finishing her breakfast the next morning that Selim Bey, the hotel proprietor, announced that there was a lady waiting in his private sanctuary to see her. Linsie frowned at him curiously for a moment. 'To see me?' she asked. 'Is it one of the ladies I was with yesterday, Selim Bey?'

Selim Bey shook his head vigorously in denial and

waved his hands. 'No, no, *hanim*, this is a lady.' He laid particular stress on the word, and used his great hands again to convey his meaning. 'This is a European lady.' He prided himself on his mastery of languages. 'Italian, I think, *hanim*.'

'Italian!' Linsie was on her feet in a moment, her heart suddenly racing wildly, though for no good reason really except that she could think of only one Italian lady that she had met recently. 'I'm coming, Selim Bey, thank you.' She turned in the doorway and looked back at him. 'Oh, if you see Mr. Lemiz will you ask him to join us, please?' she said, and Selim Bey bowed agreement, although he also looked vaguely puzzled.

It was the same woman, there was no doubt. That fair hair going grey and those bright blue eyes with their gentle enquiring expression, so different from her son's hard ones. She extended a hand as Linsie came towards her and smiled a little apologetically.

'I hope I did not disturb you, *signorina*,' she said in that soft, faintly accented voice. 'I am the Contessa Contini—there was no time yesterday to introduce myself.'

Linsie willingly accepted the long, slim hand that was proffered and smiled. 'I'm Linsie Palmer,' she said. Yesterday she had liked the woman instinctively and today was no different, although the title was somewhat of a surprise, she had to admit.

'Miss Palmer.' She accepted the offer of a chair, although Linsie thought she looked a little apprehensive about her surroundings. She sat for a second

43

with her elegant hands in her lap and her eyes not quite meeting Linsie's. 'I came mostly, Miss Palmer, to correct the impression you may have of my son,' she went on in the same soft voice, and Linsie raised a questioning brow.

It was impossible to imagine that Celik Demaril himself knew anything of this visit or he would surely have forbidden it. Celik Demaril was not the kind of man to offer explanations to anyone about his behaviour, and certainly not to a foreign female journalist whom he had forcibly evicted from his property. Therefore the Contessa's visit was even more puzzling.

'I don't think I was allowed long enough to form any impression of Mr. Demaril,' Linsie said. 'I saw him for only a few minutes, Contessa.'

The Contessa's blue eyes clouded slightly and she drew her fine brows into a small frown, shaking her head slowly. 'It was most unfortunate that you chose such a way to—to approach my son,' she told her, gently chiding. 'He has such an intense dislike of having his privacy invaded.'

Unwilling to appear quite without scruples, Linsie shook her head and set about explaining her reasons. 'It's very important to me, this assignment,' she said. 'And I tried to make an appointment to see Mr. Demaril, but he refused to even consider it. Before that I'd tried to contact him by telephone, only to have the exchange refuse to give me the number or even put me through.'

'It is necessary to keep it private,' the Contessa

told her, sounding vaguely apologetic about it.

'Getting in the way I did was the only other way I could see open to me,' Linsie told her as patiently as she could. 'I'm a journalist, Contessa Contini, and I have a story to print about Mr. Demaril—personal contact is the only way I can produce that story.'

The Contessa's gentle face looked briefly sad and she waved elegant, fluttery hands. 'You gained such an—an unfortunate impression of him,' she said. 'It was such a pity.'

It was becoming increasingly clear to Linsie why the Contessa had come all the way down here to see her, and she wondered what kind of a journalist she imagined her to be. 'I work for a very respectable women's magazine,' she told her quietly. 'I can only print what I find, Contessa. If you could persuade Mr. Demaril to see me, it would mean a lot to me.'

The Contessa, however, was already shaking her head even before Linsie finished speaking. 'I could not do that, Miss Palmer,' she said with a trace of regret. 'My son does not distinguish between one journalist and another—he would never consent to see you now that he knows your profession. If only something could have been arranged without his knowing of it——' She spread her slender hands in resignation. 'It was a long time ago, when we were living in Italk, Celik and I, shortly after his father died, he had some rather unhappy experiences, and coming at such a time——'

Linsie looked vaguely started. 'Experiences with the Press?' she asked, and the Contessa nodded. It was plain to Linsie that whatever she had in mind to tell her would not come easily.

'There were so many things all together,' she said, as if she sought carefully for words. 'First Celik's father died and then—then I remarried. It was unfortunate,' she went on hastily, as if Linsie had a right to an explanation, 'but one does not always consider——' The slender shoulders again expressed far more than words could, and Linsie wondered just how condemning her son had been about her remarriage.

'Celik was also *my* father's heir, you will understand,' she said, 'and when his grandfather died so soon afterwards, the Press found him an irresistible target. He disliked it intensely, always being followed and photographed, but he was suddenly one of the richest young men in the world and he was—interesting, you see.'

'Yes, I see.' Linsie saw only too well and she sympathised, but she also saw that getting her interview was going to be even harder than she had anticipated, and for a moment her heart felt hopelessly heavy.

'When—when things failed, we came back to Turkey.' The Contessa seemed anxious to reveal every possible reason for her son's reluctance to cooperate, and Linsie hadn't the heart to show disinterest. 'Celik was happier here, and I too love the country and the people. I tell you all this, Miss Palmer,' she emphasised, 'so that you may understand my son's dislike of newspaper reporters. It is not a personal dislike of you only.'

46

'Oh no, of course not, I understand.'

Linsie almost yielded to one of her impulses and decided to go home and forget all about it. Almost, but not quite, for she remembered how hard she had fought to be given this assignment, and her pride refused to let her go back home empty-handed, no matter if she did sympathise with her quarry.

It was at that moment that Kadri appeared, sent in by Selim Bey as she had requested, and she introduced him to the Contessa, noting his curious frown when he was told who the visitor was. 'Contessa Contini says it is most unlikely that Mr. Demaril will ever change his mind and see me, now that he knows I'm a journalist,' Linsie told him, and felt a twinge of annoyance because he looked so obviously relieved.

'I am very sorry to hear that,' he murmured politely, and Linsie almost betrayed his insincerity with a disbelieving laugh. He looked at her with a glimmer of speculation in his dark eyes, as if he wondered what she would do next. 'You will now return with me to Istanbul, Linsie, and visit for a while before going home?' he suggested, and Linsie shrugged, unwilling to say too much about her future plans in front of the Contessa.

'I'll see,' she told him non-committally. 'I rather like it in Antalya and I think I'll spend some time here before I think of going home. But you go home by all means, Kadri, if you want to.'

'And leave you here alone?' He looked quite scandalised at the idea, and the Contessa too looked vaguely uneasy, though whether for the same reasons was doubtful.

'It would not be very wise of you to remain here alone, Miss Palmer,' she suggested in her gentle voice. 'The Turks are a very hospitable people, as I have reason to know, but there are certain customs that take a long time to change.' She looked at Kadri, seeking his help, almost certain she would find it. 'If it was possible I would gladly invite you to stay at the villa, but——' She shrugged expressive shoulders, and Linsie almost smiled when she imagined Celik Demaril's stern, angry face should his mother have the effrontery to return with the hated journalist as a house guest.

'No, of course it isn't possible, Contessa,' she said. 'But it's quite comfortable here at the inn, and Selim Bey's an excellent host. I shall stay for a while at least.'

There seemed nothing else to say, but the Contessa still seemed oddly reluctant to leave it there. She sat for a moment longer with her slender hands flutteringly restless in her lap, a small anxious frown between her fine brows, then she looked at Linsie anxiously.

'The—the writing you are to do about my son, Miss Palmer?' she enquired softly. 'What will you say? I am anxious, you will understand, that there is nothing adverse printed about him. It would be most unkind and quite untrue if you were to make your impression of him yesterday public.'

It took Linsie some seconds to decide just how to

answer and she could feel not only the Contessa's anxious gaze on her but also Kadri's curious one. 'For the moment,' she decided at last, 'I'll leave the matter of the interview—I'll decide later whether or not to abandon it completely. It's something I don't like doing, but if Mr. Demaril refuses to see me, I suppose I haven't much choice.'

'I am sorry.'

The apology was so softly spoken and obviously so genuine that Linsie was touched, and in one of her uncontrollably impulsive gestures she leaned across and touched the Contessa's hand. 'So am I,' she said ruefully.

The Contessa got up from the hard chair with an elegant grace and she looked much less anxious, Linsie was glad to see. She extended a slim hand and she was smiling, if somewhat uncertainly. 'I hope you will believe me when I say how pleased I am that you have agreed to drop the matter,' she said in her soft voice. 'Celik—my son is not a harsh man, although he may have given you that impression, Miss Palmer, but he has this—this attitude towards journalists, and he hates to have his home invaded. It is, you will agree, reasonable.'

'I suppose it is,' Linsie admitted reluctantly, and already saw her precious interview as a thing that might have been. The Contessa Contini was far too persuasive.

'You will not write an—an unkind piece about my son?' she insisted softly, and Linsie shook her head, wondering how she had managed to allow herself to be so persuaded.

Celik Demaril's angry harshness had made her only the more determined to track him down, but the Contessa with her gentle, persuasive voice had brought her to the brink of agreeing to forget the whole thing and go home. Not that she had committed herself verbally, but she had so nearly done so, and no doubt Kadri would see her present attitude as surrender.

'I won't write anything that isn't true, Contessa,' she promised. 'It wouldn't be—ethical.'

For a moment she caught a fleeting glimpse of anxiety in the Contessa's blue eyes again, but then she smiled and once more extended her hand. 'I trust you, Miss Palmer,' she said softly. 'I hope that we may see one another again some time.'

'I hope so,' Linsie agreed, and once again felt a very genuine liking for the older woman. How she had managed to bear a son as harsh and unrelenting as Celik Demaril was beyond her comprehension, but perhaps he took after his Turkish father.

When the Contessa had departed and the sound of her car faded into the distance, Kadri looked at Linsie for a moment, then raised a querying brow. 'Do you really mean to give up this wild goose chase?' he asked, and she did not answer for a moment. Much as she would hate to do anything to hurt the Contessa, she still had an obligation to try and interview Celik Demaril and also her own pride was at stake.

'I didn't say I was giving up,' she pointed out carefully. 'I simply said I wouldn't print anything that wasn't true.'

'Then what will you write?' Kadri demanded, and she shrugged .

'I don't know until I can speak to him properly,' she said. 'I meant what I said about spending some time here, Kadri. I like it here and I don't have to hurry away simply because Celik Demaril isn't immediately approachable.' Her soft mouth curved into a meaningful smile that Kadri viewed with obvious suspicion. 'As I've said before,' she reminded him, 'there are more ways of killing a cat than choking it to death with butter.'

'I wish,' Kadri said with feeling, 'that you would dispose of this cat quickly and let us go back to Istanbul!'

It was very much against Kadri's inclination to let Linsie go off on her own in the ramshackle old car that Selim Bey allowed them to hire from him, but she had insisted that she felt like a drive on her own and since she was doing no more than motor a little way along the coast to Perge there was absolutely no need for her to have an escort.

Perge was quite a popular call for tourists, although she hoped to find it not too well populated today, for she was not in the mood for crowds. Selim Bey, too, had doubts about her going off alone, but she had eventually defied the opinion of both of them and driven off in the ancient car, determined to enjoy herself.

To get to Perge, in fact, it was necessary to drive inland, for the excellent modern road actually ran some distance in from the shore and through the foothills of the Taurus mountains. She was feeling quite elated with anticipation as she drove eastwards out of Antalya and it was not long before she was driving through a lushly fertile area that seemed to consist mainly of numerous smallholdings.

There were orange, lemon and grapefruit growing in abundance and groves of grey, twisty olive trees, and the scent of the millions of blossoms was quite heady in its effect. Then as the fruit groves were left behind and the land levelled out she found herself driving through a vast open plain with the sea somewhere out of sight on her right and the soaring beauty of the Taurus mountains on her left. Snow-capped peaks and dark swathes of forest swept down to the foothills and were breathtaking in their beauty.

Low stone walls divided the plain into fields of various sizes where tractors were preparing the ground for sowing and long lines of tall, slim cypresses waved elegantly against the blue sky. As she drove further the hills were closer to the road and she could see how oddly shaped they were—some quite flattened on top, some rounded and smooth and others ragged and peaked, but all covered in dark, lush pine forests that gave only glimpses of the molten silver waterfalls that sped down from the mountain snows.

There was so much to see and admire that she almost missed the turning she wanted to take that would bring her to Perge. A village lay around the turning that led into the foothills and she so nearly missed her turning that she gave the wheel a sharp twist and bounced off the edge of the road into the wall of a cottage.

It must have been the lower edge of the windscreen that struck her forehead as she was thrown forward, but she knew nothing about the silence that followed her car's violent crunch against the white wall of the house, or the minutes that followed when no one was about and the sun beat down on her defenceless head.

She vaguely recalled a voice exclaiming in Turkish as she briefly recovered consciousness, but then she wafted off again and the soft voice was lost.

'*Merek etmeyin.*'

That voice too was Turkish, it was also vaguely familiar, but the coolness of water on her forehead was far too pleasant a sensation for her to bother about anything else at the moment. She was somewhere in the shade too, somewhere that smelled vaguely like a kitchen, but it was blessedly cool and she had no desire to care about that either.

'Miss Palmer!'

The voice was very definitely familiar, and she flicked her eyelashes briefly in surprise without actually opening her eyes. The last time she had heard that voice it had been ordering her in no uncertain manner to leave the garden at Farik, the house in the hills. Another deliciously cool sensation was again pressed to her forehead, and again the voice intruded insistently into her half consciousness.

'Miss Palmer!'

She opened her eyes at last and looked up at him. The stern dark features looked even darker in the shadows of the long, low room and the blue eyes were searching her face in a way that surely could not have been anxious. One long brown hand was pressed to her cheek as she opened her eyes and hastily withdrawn when he saw that she was conscious again.

On the other side of her a woman, kneeling, her face half hidden by the lower half of her headcloth, kindly dark eyes watching her anxiously from above it, and one hand holding the dampened cloth to her forehead. Linsie spared her a smile and a swift curious glance before looking back to Celik Demaril, who now rose from the semi-crouched position he had been in when she first opened her eyes.

'I am glad that you are recovered,' he told her in his pedantic English. 'As I see that you are travelling without a hat I assume that you fainted with the heat and crashed your car.'

It was ridiculous to want to laugh in the circumstances, but somehow Linsie almost did. Here she was laid out unconscious in some strange house and all he could summon in the way of comfort was a rather offhand opinion that she was responsible for her own predicament for being without a hat.

He stood over her, seeming gigantic in the low-ceilinged room and his face all but indiscernible in the shadows now. Only those blue eyes clearly identifiable as they glittered down at her, almost as if he resented her being here as much as on his own property.

He wore no jacket, but a cream shirt that clung to that sinewy frame like a second skin and showed the golden brown skin through its texture. Fawn trousers hugged his lean hips and fitted smoothly over long, powerful-looking legs, his feet planted firmly apart on the rough floor of the peasant house with an arrogance that made it appear as if he owned both them and it. The woman was obviously impressed, for she kept her eyes shyly downcast.

'My hat must have come off when the car crashed,' Linsie told him, and was surprised to find how faint and whispery her voice sounded. 'The heat had nothing to do with it—I simply turned too sharply, that's all.'

The frown that drew his dark brows together made him look even more forbidding, and she lay there looking up at him, feeling rather at his mercy and strangely vulnerable. 'You are alone?' he asked.

He made it sound like an accusation and she knew he would not approve any more than Kadri did, but he would have even less hesitation in saying so. 'I came for a drive on my own,' she said, sounding deliberately offhand. 'I wanted to see Perge, and that sort of thing isn't really in Kadri's line.'

'The young man who was with you when you came to Farik the first time?' he asked, and again she felt a small niggle of resentment as being cross-questioned.

She nodded, nevertheless. 'My photographer.'

'Hmm!'

He somehow managed to convey a great deal with the wordless sound, and Linsie decided that it was time she sat up and let him know that she was not simply prepared to lie there and let him walk rough-shod all over her. She smiled at the woman who still held a cool, damp cloth to her forehead, and sat up with as much grace as she could muster in the circumstances.

The woman looked anxious when she swayed slightly, but she smiled at her reassuringly and sat for a moment on the edge of the rough, skin-covered pallet bed. Once her legs felt less weak and trembly she intended getting to her feet without assistance, but before she could do so, two large strong hands reached down for hers and she was drawn to her feet.

For a brief moment she stood in close proximity to him and she was quite appalled to notice the way her pulses were racing while those long fingers were curled about her own small hands, engulfing them in a firm, masculine warmth that sent tingles of sensation along her spine.

He released her slowly, and his fingers slid away with an almost sensual reluctance that surprised her. 'Your head is slightly injured,' he informed her coolly, 'but not badly enough to need medical attention, I think. You were fortunate not to have been more badly hurt.'

Fully aware of the fact, Linsie put an exploratory hand to her throbbing head and winced when her fingers found a small bump above her right eye, just below the hairline. 'It hurts,' she complained. 'I must have hit it on the windscreen.' She looked up at him, half accusing. 'Are you sure it doesn't need something on it?'

'I am quite sure,' he told her firmly. 'But if you have doubts then of course you must see a doctor.'

'Oh no, I—I haven't really!' She gently touched the bump on her forehead again. 'I suppose it isn't too bad.'

'Are you not as—tough as you would have one believe, *hanim*?' he asked softly, and Linsie detected sarcasm, though she thought better of saying so.

'I don't want to make a fuss,' she said in a quiet little voice. 'I'll be all right.'

'You will, of course, return to Antalya with me,' he decreed in a firm, quiet voice, and Linsie stared at him.

'I—I will?' she asked huskily.

'Of course, it is the most sensible thing to do, you are not fit to drive yourself.' It was, of course, the most sensible thing to do, but Linsie's head was aching abominably and she was not thinking very sensibly.

'Oh, but I can't!' she objected, without stopping to think.

It was quite idiotic of her to raise objections, she realised, when the chance to travel back with him to Antalya was offered like a heaven-sent opportunity, but she was suddenly strangely reluctant to take advantage of it and her head did ache so.

One dark brow was already questioning her refusal and she could guess that he saw her as a strange creature of contradictions. At one moment she was pursuing him, relentlessly determined to speak to him, and the next she was refusing to let him drive her back to Antalya and achieve the much sought after interview without even trying.

'You do not wish to return to Antalya?' he asked, and there was more than a hint of impatience in the cool voice that the watching woman recognised, if Linsie didn't. She was looking at her with a definite glint of warning in her dark eyes.

'Yes, of course I want to get back,' Linsie told him. 'But the car I'm—I was driving belongs to Selim Bey at the inn, and I ought to——'

'The car is not fit to drive at the moment,' he interrupted shortly. 'And I suggest that you are not fit to drive either, Miss Palmer. You will be wise to accept my offer and return with me.' The startling blue eyes glittered meaningly. 'I am sure that your companion will understand the circumstances.'

Th implication was veiled, but it was there, and Linsie felt a warm flush of colour in her face as she looked up at him, a bright sparkle of indignation in her own eyes. 'I'm not sure *I* understand,' she told him in a slightly shaky voice. 'I can't think how you came to be here, or why you should concern yourself with one of the journalists you profess to despise so much.'

He took the retort with a tight-lipped look that promised a hot temper, and she was prepared to see

58

him walk out of the cottage and leave her to her own devices. Instead he held her reluctant gaze for a moment, then looked at her hastily lowered head with a scornful arrogance that she could feel even without seeing it.

'You are a guest in my country, Miss Palmer,' he said in a firm cool voice that put her firmly in her place. 'I recognised you as the woman was trying to move you into shade. Much as I despise your profession, I would not willingly see you suffer as Europeans can suffer in our climate.'

A new and quite disturbing realisation dawned on Linsie then, and she cast him a swift, curious glance from the depth of her lashes. 'You—you carried me up here?' she asked with uncharacteristic meekness, and he looked as if he would like to deny it.

'It was necessary to give you shade,' he said in a short, reluctant admission. 'If you are feeling able, Miss Palmer, we will be on our way—you can collect your hat on the way if it is in the car as you say.'

'Thank you.' There seemed little else to say, and she again looked at the waiting, watching woman, her dark eyes following the exchange almost as well as if she could understand the words they spoke. 'I'd like to thank her——' she said, and he nodded shortly.

He spoke to the woman in Turkish and her hostess smiled, her eyes, above the rough veil, bright in her country brown face. Without another word he turned and strode out of the door, ducking his head to avoid the low lintel, and clattering down the wooden outside staircase and Linsie, after another smile for her

59

rescuer, followed him more cautiously.

She turned back to see the woman smiling warmly and sending meaningful glances at Celik Bey's departing back as he crossed the yard to his car. She appeared to be finding something very amusing, and Linsie thought she could guess something of what was going through her mind. She smiled and waved a hand, nothing loath to have the woman speculate, as long as Celik Demaril knew nothing about it.

'*Güle-güle!*' the woman called softly, and Linsie nodded, even though she had no idea what the words meant—but they sounded friendly.

CHAPTER FOUR

KADRI was looking at her curiously and Linsie wished she could make more sense of her explanation. Why she had so lacked initiative during her drive back from Perge with Celik Demaril and not taken advantage of the opportunity it presented was still a sore point with her.

'But what *did* you say to him?' Kadri asked, and Linsie shrugged, using her fork to extract a morsel of meat from her plate of *türlü*. Selim Bey's wife had been a little too generous with the garlic in this instance, and the mess of meat, onions, tomatoes and herbs was not as much to her taste as usual.

'I said very little,' she said. 'For one thing I didn't feel like talking, I was—stunned, a bit dazed still, and anyway, he wasn't exactly in a chatty mood.'

'You did not attempt to interview him?' Kadri insisted, and she frowned impatiently, putting down her fork and pushing the half empty plate away with a grimace of dislike.

'No, I didn't,' she told him. 'I've said, Kadri, I was still stunned, not quite myself, and I didn't feel like walking all the way back to Antalya. You know what he's like—if I'd made just one move toward sounding like a journalist, if I'd felt like it, he'd have stopped the car at the roadside and tipped me out. He's quite capable of it!'

'You were really feeling so ill?' he asked, now looking anxious, and she nodded.

'I felt awful,' she said. 'And not in the least like interviewing anyone, least of all, Celik Demaril.'

'You do not like the man,' Kadri stated, as if it was a newly discovered fact, and Linsie laughed shortly.

'I haven't had much cause to like him so far,' she reminded him. 'Although I must say he seemed very genuinely concerned that I should get back here safely.'

'But you still think he would have—tipped you out?' he asked, carefully quoting her own words.

'Oh, I don't know!'

She shrugged again, a little irritably, and wished she did not feel quite so much as if she had failed

Kadri by not making the most of her chances with their quarry, but she really hadn't felt up to it with her head aching abominably and her hat fitting in just the wrong place to be comfortable. She contemplated the half-consumed meal on her discarded plate and frowned thoughtfully, while Kadri went on eating.

'How will you see him again?' he asked, and she shook her head.

'I don't know.' She twirled a spoon round and round between her fingers, not looking at him while she spoke. 'I still think that stowing away on his yacht is a good idea,' she ventured, and heard his sharp intake of breath as he almost choked on the last of his *türlü*.

'Linsie, you cannot do that!'

'So you say,' Linsie replied calmly. 'But I still think it would be possible, and he couldn't very well throw me overboard once we were at sea, could he?'

'You said yourself that he was capable of throwing you out of his car,' Kadri reminded her. 'Why should he hesitate to do so at sea?'

'And let me drown?' she asked scornfully. 'I don't think even a millionaire can get away with murder, can he?' She stroked her bottom lip thoughtfully for several seconds while Kadri, more or less resigned to her doing something outrageous, finished his meal. 'I suppose he takes masses of pretty girls on those jaunts in his yacht,' she guessed, and Kadri looked blank for a moment, his Muslim upbringing rebelling at the idea of unlimited orgies at sea.

'I should think it unlikely,' he told her, after a moment or two. 'He did not seem to be a promiscuous man.'

'Oh, all millionaire playboys have hordes of girls on their yachts,' she claimed extravagantly. 'Everyone knows that. It's part of the cult of being a millionaire!'

'You sound very knowledgeable,' Kadri accused, and she laughed.

'Oh, I don't speak from experience,' she told him, half teasing. 'But I do read the Sunday papers! I'm sure no one would notice an extra female aboard if I smuggled myself on early, before the rest got there.'

'It is most unwise,' Kadri warned, and she made a short impatient sound with her mouth that he regarded unfavourably. 'Also I think your father would not permit you to do such a thing,' he told her. 'I am acting on his behalf, Linsie Hanim, and I say that it is not right for you to attempt to smuggle yourself aboard this man's yacht.'

'But I have to get this interview somehow,' Linsie pleaded. 'You know how important it is to me, Kadri.'

'I know that you are trying to be something that you are not,' Kadri said quietly, not looking at her, and she frowned at him curiously.

'What *do* you mean?' she asked, and he looked up at her and smiled, shaking his head slowly.

'You try so hard to be the—the hard-boiled reporter, Linsie,' he said softly. 'But it is not you—this ruthless, determined young woman who will stop at nothing is not you, it is a mask that you put on because you wish to be thought hard and experienced.'

For a moment Linsie said nothing. It was rather disconcerting to have her character so expertly dissected, and she studied her hands for a moment as they restlessly twirled the spoon round and round. Perhaps she did try too hard to be the son that her father had always wanted to follow him into the business, but it took a keen mind to see behind her façade, and she had not given Kadri credit for being so astute.

'You don't know me,' she said quietly at last, then raised her eyes and deliberately challenged his opinion with a long, hard look. 'I'll get that interview, you'll see.'

'Regardless of what you have to do to get it?' Kadri asked, and she hastily looked away again.

'Of course, I'm a journalist! And please don't try and act like a Victorian father, Kadri, and spoil it for me. I won't get hurt or anything, but there's a good chance I'll get my interview at last.'

Kadri's dark and appealing eyes looked at her across the table, trying one last time to change her mind. 'You will not listen to me?' he asked, and she shook her head, although she wished he could have been more enthusiastic. She would have felt so much better doing it with his support.

'I need this interview, Kadri.'

Kadri sighed deeply and shook his head again, his dark eyes glistening with some inner warmth as he looked at her, his long slim hands held together in front of his face, palm to palm, almost like a prayer. 'I do not pretend to understand you, Linsie,' he said, 'but I know that you are not very easy to oppose, and I know that I am not nearly firm enough with you, as your father would wish.' His eyes lingered for a moment on her mouth and he smiled. 'You are a dangerous woman, Linsie Hanim,' he said softly.

It was rather mean of her to sneak off on her own, Linsie supposed, while Kadri was making a long telephone call to his father, but she felt like going for a walk on her own and Kadri's constant and protective company, no matter how well intentioned, was inclined to make her feel claustrophobic sometimes. What was more she suspected that the call concerned her, and she had no wish to be called to account by Kadri's father.

Antalya was a charming and attractive old town and she had never really explored it in the way she wanted to. There were any number of street hawkers, for one thing, and she wanted to listen to their cries, even if she couldn't understand what they were saying, and perhaps buy something without Kadri warning her of sharp practice.

Once away from the hotel she decided to try one of the delightful horse-drawn *paytons* that abounded in the town streets. The driver raised no objection to her being unaccompanied, as she half expected, but saw her safely into the smart, brilliant red carriage with brass lamps and highly polished hubs that gleamed in the sun. She felt rather grand and old-fashioned as they made their leisurely way along, sounding a tinkling little bell to warn of their coming.

She had no special destination in mind and managed to convey to her driver that she wanted to see some of the town and not go anywhere in particular, something he seemed quite happy to do. The sun was warm and there was a breath of warm wind off the sea, and Linsie sat back and enjoyed herself as the steady little Anatolian ponies jogged along at a pace that was almost sleep-inducing, had it not been for the things there were to see.

Her driver evidently saw her as a student of the antique, for he took her to the old part of the town, pointing his whip at various points of interest as they went, although lack of a communal language barred her from knowing exactly what it was she was looking at. But it was all very picturesque and quite enchanting, and she was enjoying it enormously.

Steep, narrow roads climbed the cliffs above the harbour, where old houses had deep, jutting bay windows that hung so far over the narrow streets that in places they almost met above the cobbled roads and gave shade to passers-by. An occasional fleeting glimpse of cool dark interiors added to the general air of peace and tranquillity, and she felt she could have spent all day there.

High walls and shady, pale-leafed plane trees gave it a faintly mystic air and everywhere the sound of running water that was such a feature of Antalya cooled the mind and suggested mountain streams and cool winds. She was actually sorry when the ride came to an end and her driver apparently enquired if she had enjoyed herself. She conveyed her pleasure as well as she could, and he departed, smiling broadly and waving his whip in farewell.

On foot once more she looked at the wares of street hawkers, revelling in the exotic strangeness of it all. A man selling balloons had a cloud of his multi-coloured wares floating way above his head and she was tempted by a childish urge to have one, and a water-seller offered ice-cold refreshment from a huge beaten brass container festooned with vine leaves.

But despite the temptations Linsie resisted and decided instead to refresh herself at one of the many outdoor *gazinos*. These were somewhat similar to the familiar Continental café, but the one she chose was situated in a small park surrounded by trees.

She felt strangely conspicuous, being alone, but determinedly defied curiosity and chose a table near the edge of those set out under the shade of pine trees. She was about to sit down when she was aware that someone had called her name quite close at hand, and she turned, frowning curiously.

The table set just behind hers and half hidden by one of the tall pines had two men seated at it when she first turned, but one of them immediately rose and hastily departed without a backward glance, even before she identified Celik Demaril as the other one.

She felt her breath catch in her throat for a moment as she met the bright challenging look in the blue eyes, and then he was getting to his feet with a

67

lazy, indolent grace that affected her senses strangely.

'You are alone still, Miss Palmer?' he asked quietly, and Linsie nodded.

Several pairs of eyes were watching her, she was well aware, and she guessed they were probably trying to guess who the woman was that Celik Bey was honouring with his company. A European woman, of course; he would never have accosted one of his own countrywomen in that way.

Linsie felt she had little option but to accept when he indicated that she should join him, and she sat down on the chair that his former companion had so hastily vacated. She wondered uneasily what he was trying to do making such a public approach, but to argue with him or refuse to accept the invitation would have made her more conspicuous than ever.

He was a strange man, she decided a little dizzily. First he went to great pains to avoid seeing her, even to the extent of removing her forcibly from his property, and now he was making advances to her in a public place. Perhaps he saw himself as her rescuer, for a second time, for it was pretty certain that she would have attracted some very odd glances if she had sat there for very long alone.

'I rather like being alone sometimes,' she said as she carefully tucked her skirt under her knees, to give her hands something to do and to stop them shaking so much.

A waiter was hovering and Celik Demaril looked at her enquiringly. 'What would you like to drink?' he asked, and she gazed at him for a moment, totally unprepared for him to go to such lengths.

'I—I don't know,' she admitted. 'I hadn't thought about it, I'm not used to——' Briefly she looked at him through her lashes. 'Can you suggest something, Mr. Demaril?'

She knew little about Turkish food and drink and usually left it to Kadri to choose what she had, but she thought he was unprepared for her asking his assistance. Briefly she could have sworn that she detected a glimpse of amusement in his eyes, but his features were still solemnly composed and he gave serious consideration to her question.

'Do you like our Turkish wines?' he asked, and she nodded, wondering what she was letting herself in for. Kadri knew something of her tastes, but Celik Demaril was different—he knew nothing about her. In the order he gave the waiter, however, she recognised the name *Marmara*, which she remembered as a full red wine, quite to her taste. Seeing her look he raised a brow. 'You know it?' he asked.

'I've had it before,' she said, and hastily added, 'I like it, thank you.'

He said nothing more until the waiter brought her wine and then merely raised a questioning brow again, presumably to ask if it was to her taste. The quiet hum of voices, softened in the open air, had almost a soporific effect and she felt suddenly and blandly relaxed, the wine smooth and rich on her palate. Maybe Celik Demaril wasn't such an ogre after all.

'You like my country?' he asked suddenly, and she

took a moment or two to answer.

'I like it very much,' she said at last, and again glanced through her lashes at the dark, strongly defined features. 'You call Turkey your country?' she asked, and saw the swift dark frown draw his brows together.

'That is a curious question, Miss Palmer,' he said in a cool, quiet voice. 'I do not think I quite understand it.'

Trying not to be deterred by his obvious resentment, Linsie put her elbows on the little table and looked at him steadily. If she was ever to get that interview, now was as good a time as any, and it could be said that it was of his own choosing, since he had invited her to join him.

'I've met the Contessa Contini,' she told him, wondering, too late, if she was betraying a confidence by telling him that. 'Your mother being Italian, I wondered if you thought of yourself as belonging to either race completely.'

'I am Turkish,' he informed her flatly, and again she was subjected to the scrutiny of those very unTurkish blue eyes.

'Actually——' She was anxious to go on as fast as possible now that she had at least a chance of achieving her object. 'I was rather surprised to see that the Contessa was fair-haired and blue-eyed, and your own eyes——' She met them head-on briefly, then swiftly looked away again, finding the contact too disturbing to prolong it. 'I thought Italians were mostly dark,' she finished lamely, and curled her

70

fingers into her palms when he gave a short, harsh laugh.

'My mother is from northern Italy, Miss Palmer,' he said, and sounded as if he despaired of her intelligence. 'It is not uncommon for the people in that part of the country to have fair hair and blue eyes.'

Seldom had she felt so small and chastened and Linsie wished fervently that the ground would open up and swallow her. Why had she not checked facts like that before she got this far? It was no excuse that Kadri did not know either, for it was not Kadri's job to know such things, it was hers, she was the journalist.

'I'm—I'm sorry,' she said, and tried not to sound as if it mattered too much. 'I didn't know.'

'Evidently!'

She felt the colour warm in her cheeks and wanted to hit out in her frustration. It seemed she was never to get the better of Celik Demaril, no matter what methods she tried.

'It's usually taken for granted that Italians are dark,' she declared in her own defence, but her excuse made little impression, that was obvious.

He leaned with one elbow on the table, holding his glass of wine, and the posture brought him much too close for her comfort. He wore a light fawn suit with a white shirt and a brown tie, but even in such westernised garb he looked far less like a city businessman than a dangerously attractive brigand.

His strong, craggy features were lent emphasis by the soft shade of the pines that etched in shadowy hollows and fine lines, and his mouth, wide and rather thin-lipped, looked cruel, like the glitter in those blue eyes as they regarded her. Dark brows, up-turned slightly at their outer corners, added a further suggestion of eastern mystery and even his brown hair took on a more sable darkness in the shadows.

He was disturbing, and Linsie wanted suddenly to be away from him, interview or not, but even while she was seeking for reasons for a hasty departure, he was speaking again. 'Do you always walk around strange towns unaccompanied, Miss Palmer?' he asked softly, and she flicked him a swift, uneasy glance through her lashes.

'It isn't unusual in England, or indeed in most European countries, for women to walk wherever they please, unaccompanied,' she told him, although he must surely know it already. 'Your customs might be suitable here, Mr. Demaril, but they're very restricting and they wouldn't suit European tastes.'

'You like your—freedom?'

The question was unexpected and she looked at him curiously for a moment. 'Yes—yes, of course I do,' she said. 'It's natural to me.'

'As it would seem natural to me that you should be protected and not exposed to risk each time you leave your home.'

Linsie was finding the conversation oddly intimate, and she stirred uneasily on her chair, her hands clasped together round the stem of the wine glass. 'I don't need protection,' she told him in a rather small voice that held a trace of uncertainty.

72

'You have no fear of going anywhere alone?'

His insistence was puzzling, perhaps even disturbing, she could not yet decide. Nodding a little vaguely, she shrugged. 'Within reason, of course,' she said.

He shook his head slowly, as if it was beyond his comprehension. 'Either you are a very brave young woman, or a very foolish one,' he said. 'I cannot at the moment decide which.'

'I'm neither,' Linsie denied, prepared to defend her right to freedom, even at the risk of offending him. 'I'd be little use at my job, Mr. Demaril, if I was afraid of going about alone.'

'Your job?' One dark brow gave doubt to the description, and Linsie bit down an instinctive resentment for his opinion.

'I'm good at my job, Mr. Demaril,' she said. 'Given a chance I'd be *very* good.'

'And you consider I have denied you that chance?'

She hesitated to be quite so outspoken, but it was true, and she wanted him to know how important that interview was to her. 'I—I think you could have co-operated,' she said, choosing words carefully. 'But I can still write a feature, even though you refuse to be interviewed.' A raised brow questioned the ethics of that, but he said nothing for the moment. 'I have an outline,' Linsie went on, 'and what I don't actually know I can hazard a guess at.'

'I see.'

'For instance, I know you have a yacht,' she went on, in a voice that sounded increasingly thin and nervous. 'I can visualise the parties on board, the people, dancing, all the usual trimmings that go with a millionaire's yacht.'

'You can?' He had taken a long flat Turkish cigarette from a case and he bent his head over it while he applied the flame of a gold lighter to its tip. There was something about him, about the way he spoke in that cool, quiet voice that trickled a shiver of warning along her spine.

'Of course I *wouldn't*,' she said a little breathlessly. 'I mean, there must be—there must be other ways of ——' She spread her hands wide in a curiously appealing gesture. 'I wouldn't,' she insisted.

He drew on the cigarette and its pungent smoke tickled her nostrils pleasantly, then he raised the glass of wine to his lips and drained it in one long draught. He put the glass down carefully on the table and Linsie watched in fascination the long strength of his fingers.

'I am sailing for Side the day following tomorrow,' he said quietly and matter-of-factly. 'If you would care to accompany me, Miss Palmer, you would see for yourself what goes on on my yacht.'

Linsie swallowed hard, trying not to let her mouth drop open as it felt inclined to do, her eyes wide and incredulous in the pale oval of her face. 'You— you're asking me to sail with you?' she asked, and cleared her throat hastily when she heard her own voice, soft and husky.

'Is that not what you wanted?' he asked, drawing again on the cigarette and sending the resulting

74

smoke in an effective screen before his face.

The little *gazino* seemed suddenly to have become even more quiet and she could almost imagine that every customer was listening, waiting to hear what her answer would be. Her pulses were pounding, jerkily erratic, at her temple and she could feel her hands shaking as she clasped them again round the stem of her wine glass.

'I—I don't know quite what to say,' she whispered at last. 'It's—it's very—very thoughtful of you, Mr. Demaril.'

'You are accepting the invitation?'

'Yes, yes, of course, thank you!' She had no hesitation once the full meaning dawned on her.

Her interview would be in no doubt now. She would mix with the guests on his yacht, learn the kind of people he liked, mixed with socially. It was a heaven-sent opportunity and she could still hardly believe it had happened.

He leaned forward and knocked the ash from the end of his cigarette, his blue eyes for the moment concealed by thick dark lashes. 'You wished to know about me, about my hobbies, my enthusiasms,' he went on in the same quiet voice, 'this will give you the opportunity to learn just what—makes me tick?—is that right?'

'That's right!' Linsie smiled; she almost laughed aloud in her pleasure. So much for Celik Demaril being unapproachable—he was human after all, and she would be the first to admit it. She could scarcely wait to tell Kadri what she had achieved simply by sticking to her guns.

Unexpectedly, Kadri was not as wildly excited about
the prospect of her sailing with Celik Demaril's party
as she had hoped. In fact he looked far from pleased
about it and Linsie frowned her annoyance at his
lack of enthusiasm.

'It's exactly what I wanted, don't you see?' she
said. 'The millionaire playboy among his friends—
it's just what our readers love! Of course I'll need to
take an evening dress with me as well as trousers and
things, I must be able to mingle!'

'Linsie!' Kadri reached for her hands, the most
intimate gesture he had ever made towards her, and
held them for a moment in his own, looking at her
with those dark, persuasive eyes, anxious now and
not bright and luminous as they so often were. 'Listen
to me,' he urged. 'I do not want to spoil your enthusiasm——'

'You can't!' Linsie assured him with a shake of
her fair head. 'Nothing could—I've made it, Kadri,
and I mean to make the most of this chance!'

'I am not happy about it.'

His voice, even the way he sat so rigidly, as if he
had heard bad news and could not quite believe it.
He held her hands for a moment longer, then suddenly seemed to realise what he was doing and let
them slip from his grasp slowly, his long slim fingers
almost caressing.

'Please, Kadri!' She shook her head, something of
his uncertainty communicating itself to her, but not

for very long. 'Don't spoil it for me,' she begged. 'I know you can't come too, but I promise I'll be careful, I won't——' she pulled a face, 'I won't misbehave.'

'I know.' He spoke softly and she had never seen him so serious even when he was scolding her for not behaving with as much propriety as he thought she should. He looked at her steadily for a moment longer, then shook his head. 'I will not spoil it for you, Linsie,' he said softly. 'But please be very careful.'

Her impulse was to lean across the table and kiss him, very gently, like a very good friend, but she resisted the impulse for Kadri's sake. He would be so much more stunned by such a gesture than one of her own countrymen would have been. Instead she reached across and touched his hands lightly with her fingertips, her eyes warm and glowing softly.

'I will,' she promised. 'And thank you for worrying about me, dear Kadri.'

CHAPTER FIVE

As well as feeling more excited than she had ever done in her life before, Linsie also felt vaguely uneasy about the forthcoming trip on board Celik

Demaril's yacht, although she could think of no good reason why she should, and not for anything would she have let Kadri know how she felt.

Ever since receiving that unexpected invitation from Celik Demaril she had been trying to dwell only on the favourable possibilities of it, and dismiss any vague notions that all was not as well as it appeared. The invitation had suddenly swung things her way, and she would be a fool not to make the most of her unexpected luck.

She would be getting her much sought-after interview and her hitherto elusive quarry was ready to co-operate at last, or why else would he have invited her to join his party? She would also get a taste of the millionaire life too, and yet somehow, at the back of her mind, was the persistent certainty that something was wrong. A suspicion that there was something other than the chance of an interview and a pleasant cruise in store for her that refused to be dismissed.

She had asked Kadri something about Side, the destination that Celik Demaril had mentioned, and learned that it lay a little further round the coast from Antalya. At present it was a small and pleasant town, used to catering for visitors, but in its long-ago past it had been a thriving and prosperous port, deriving much of its prosperity from slavery and the dubious trading of pirates.

If the yacht was actually going to touch port she would find it all very interesting, Kadri assured her, but whether they would or not was one of the mysteries of the trip. It would have been a little more reassuring if she could have got in touch with her prospective host and found out a few more details about the trip, but remembering her past abortive efforts, she had little choice but to wait until she heard from him.

All the day following her meeting with Celik Demaril she expected to hear either from him or a member of his staff, giving her details, but up until breakfast on the day she had expected to go, she heard nothing, and she was feeling not only anxious but even more suspicious.

'Suppose he goes without me,' she said to Kadri. 'He might, Kadri, he might have second thoughts about taking me along.'

'I do not think so,' Kadri assured her, but it was evident from his voice that much the same thought had occurred to him, and Linsie frowned over the possibility.

'If he does——' she began, but Kadri was shaking his head.

'If he does go without you, there is nothing you can do, Linsie,' he said quietly. 'And I, for one, will be relieved if he *does* change his mind.'

'Oh, you would!' Linsie set her chin firmly against disappointment, and there was a glint in her eyes that boded ill for Celik Demaril if he had indeed decided to go without her, although she knew there was nothing she could do about it, as he said.

She had almost begun to resign herself to frustrated and angry disappointment, when Selim Bey appeared, apologised for interrupting their meal and

79

announced a message for Linsie Hanim from Celik Bey. 'The gentleman will be ready to sail in one half hour, *hanim*,' he told her, and was visibly impressed with the importance of her caller.

'Half an hour?'

Linsie stared at him in disbelief, but he nodded with every appearance of certainty. She looked across at Kadri and saw the frown that drew his dark brows together, and the gleam of doubt in his eyes. Then he spoke to Selim Bey in his own tongue, presumably making quite sure there was no misunderstanding.

Selim Bey answered in English, making it obvious that their doubt offended him. 'I am absolutely certain, *beyefendi*,' he assured Kadri. 'Celik Bey's yacht will leave harbour in one half hour.'

'Oh, that man!' Linsie was on her feet in a moment, her eyes bright with anger and determination. 'He means to go without me if I'm not there in time,' she said, 'and he thinks I can't make it!'

'But, Linsie——' Kadri attempted to reason with her, but she stood there, half-finished meal in front of her, her chin outthrust.

'Kadri, I want you to take me down there in the car!'

'Now?' He looked startled and far from happy, but she was determined not to let the opportunity slip through her fingers no matter what devious tactics Celik Demaril used.

'Now!' she insisted. 'I'm going to be there on time —he's not going to get away with trying tricks like that on me!'

Kadri looked for a moment as if he would try and find excuses, but then he merely shrugged his expressive shoulders and gave up, while Selim Bey nodded only half-conscious approval of his taking the old car, now mobile again after Linsie's minor mishap with it.

It was only minutes later that Kadri was driving her down the same steep road she had travelled in the *payton* only a couple of days before. This time, however, she spared little time or interest for her surroundings but was intent only on getting to the harbour as quickly as possible and on board the yacht that was moored there.

Some time before they got there she could see it, riding gently on the turquoise sea, and she curled her hands in her impatience as Kadri made his way down the steep narrow road to the harbour. He was driving, so it seemed to Linsie in her impatience, more cautiously than he had ever done before.

That yacht was magnificent, particularly in such a setting, white and shining in the hot sun, its gleaming brasswork and bright, cedar-coloured woodwork rich and glowing with good care. As far as they could see when they finally arrived on the quay, it looked deserted, although there was a gangway erected between the boat and the harbour, and when Kadri stopped the car they sat for a moment looking across at the gently swaying yacht in silence.

Then Linsie got out, but still stood with wide, curious eyes, looking for some sign of life, Kadri taking her small case from the boot of the car. It looked

81

curiously deserted for a pleasure craft about to sail with a party of people bent on enjoying themselves, and again she experienced that curious sense of doubt.

She could see no sign of her host, but the boat was not quite as deserted as she had first thought, for on deck was a small, leather-visaged man who was probably not as old as his lined face implied, but had his character etched deeply into his mahogany features by sun and wind as well as years.

He wore a white shirt, open at the neck, and a seaman's dark cap on the back of his grey head, with smart navy trousers completing the picture, and he looked at Linsie with narrowed eyes as she approached. His semi-uniform gave him a comfortingly familiar air somehow, reminding her of week-end sailors at home on the Thames, and she felt a little less apprehensive for a moment.

Another, younger seaman appeared and said a few words to the older man, then glanced briefly down at Linsie on the quay before going below again. Then she noticed one or two more figures darting about busily on the lower deck, all of them apparently crew members and presumably preparing for imminent departure, so that she was reminded of her own need to get aboard before they went without her.

She knew that Kadri was still standing beside the car, waiting, hoping to be able to take her back to the hotel with him, but she was firmly set against doing anything of the sort and she smiled up at the old man on the deck hopefully. If Celik Demaril had confided in anyone about her joining the party, it would surely have been in this old man, for he was evidently in authority, from his place on the upper deck.

'Good morning,' she called to him. 'My name's Linsie Palmer. I—I think Mr. Demaril is expecting me.'

For a moment he said nothing, so that she wondered if he understood English, but then he shook his head in the slightest gesture of dissent, and came forward slightly, leaning over the rail surrounding the deck, the better to be heard. 'I do not think so, *hanim*,' he told her in a voice only slightly more accented and pedantic than Celik Demaril's. 'You have made a mistake, possibly.'

Linsie stared, taken aback for the moment. 'This *is* Mr. Celik Demeril's yacht, isn't it?' she asked, and again the man nodded briefly. 'Then you *must* be expecting me,' she insisted.

'I think not, *hanim*,' he insisted politely but firmly, then broke off and shrugged his shoulders in relief when Celik Demaril himself appeared suddenly from below deck. The man said a word or two in Turkish to him, then looked again at Linsie with shrewd, speculative eyes.

His employer answered, also in their own tongue, then came to the top of the gangway and stood for a moment looking down at her with a glitter in those blue eyes that could have been resentment or exasperation or both. 'Miss Palmer,' he said coolly, 'I had not expected you so promptly.'

83

'You thought I'd be too late,' Linsie accused, still smarting under the suspected trickery. 'You *hoped* I would be!'

'Did I?' She noted the lift of his brows as if the matter was of little interest to him one way or the other, and her mouth pursed reproachfully.

'You—you had second thoughts,' she accused, rashly determined to let him know she saw through him. 'You changed your mind about letting me come and hoped by not telling me when you intended leaving until the very last minute that I'd be too late arriving!'

He said nothing in reply to the accusation, but nodded as if to dismiss the whole thing. 'Well, since you are here in time, Miss Palmer,' he said, 'you had best come aboard.'

Reaching back, Linsie took the case from Kadri's reluctant hold and gave him a brief smile before she stepped on to the gangway. Her legs felt strangely weak and there was a heavy, anxious beat in her heart that fluttered into sudden agitation when Celik Demaril extended a large hand to help her. A shudder of inexplicable excitement shivered through her when his strong fingers closed about her wrist, and she experienced also a brief sense of alarm that was surely unwarranted.

She cast a brief, uncertain glance in Kadri's direction, but he was still standing on the quay looking far from happy, and her present instinct was to run back and join him. Shaking off such traitorous instincts firmly, she turned back to Celik Demaril and caught

84

a glimpse of smile that barely touched his wide mouth but glinted in the blue eyes, and did nothing at all to reassure her.

Then he shrugged his broad shoulders carelessly. 'I had thought perhaps you would change your own mind, Miss Palmer,' he said. 'But I should have known that such a thing was unlikely, of course.'

Linsie bit back the retort that rose instinctively to her lips and instead merely shook her head slowly, and clutched tightly to her case. 'I—I told you how much this meant to me, Mr. Demaril,' she reminded him, and he nodded, his eyes now concerned with the case she carried.

'You have luggage?' he enquired coolly, and she nodded, briefly surprised.

'Just—just one or two things,' she said. 'I thought —I mean I didn't know just how long I'd be gone.'

'No more than two or three days,' he replied. 'What you are wearing would have served admirably.'

She was wearing a short, pleated white skirt and a navy tee-shirt, very nautical, Kadri had called it, and her long fair hair was tied back with a navy chiffon scarf. It was neat and attractive and she knew she looked good in it, but she could certainly not wear it continuously for the next couple of days.

She frowned at him curiously. 'But surely, Mr. Demaril——'

'If you have trousers,' he interrupted with equal coolness, 'they would be even more suitable.'

A little dazedly, Linsie nodded her head. 'I—I

85

have,' she said, still clutching her case. 'In here.'

'Then by all means bring it!' She took the opportunity at that moment to look back at Kadri and smile, but before she had a chance to say even a word to him, her host was already moving off, taking the case from her unresisting fingers and indicating with an impatient jerk of his head that she could accompany him. 'This way!' he instructed.

She had time only to wave a hand at Kadri before she was whisked below decks into the cool but rather claustrophobic confines of a passageway with several closed doors along its dim narrowness.

Down here it smelled of varnish and new wood, as it did on deck, and it seemed strangely quiet and deserted for a yacht about to sail on a pleasure cruise along the coast. Once again she briefly dwelt on the fact that it was strange to find it so bereft of the company of guests she expected, and again that quiver of apprehension shivered through her.

There was a smell of engine oil down here, too, although it took her a moment or two to recognise it for what it was, and she realised that the yacht was motor-driven and not dependent on sail. Celik Demaril, of course, would dislike being dependent on anything as unreliable as the elements.

She noticed that the ceiling overhead almost brushed the top of his head as he led the way along the narrow passageway, and she could not help noticing the breadth of his shoulders under the thin coolness of white cotton, or the muscular power in those long legs as they strode out ahead of her, fitted closely in cream cotton trousers. Rope-soled shoes deadened the sound of his footsteps and swished softly on the polished lino floor, and yet again she tried to still the vague, uneasy stirrings in her heart as she followed him.

'In here!'

Again a monosyllabic order gave her direction, and he opened the last door along the passageway as he spoke, standing aside to let her go in first, then stepping just inside to set down the case he was carrying. Watching her, waiting for a comment, she felt certain, those blue eyes steady and challenging.

The cabin was smaller than she had been expecting, and not nearly as luxurious. It was curiously masculine too, almost spartan, she would have said, but it was clean and neat and the woodwork here gleamed and shone as it did on deck. A small fitted carpet lent a touch of comfort, however, and there were curtains at the two portholes that looked out to the open sea.

'It—it's very nice.'

She turned and looked at him, still troubled by that small niggle of doubt, although there was no other reason for it than the absence of noisy chatter and the atmosphere of gaiety she would have expected from a party about to embark on a pleasure cruise.

It was possible that Celik Demaril preferred his guests to remain out of the way, of course, during the preparations to leave harbour, and there was no other cause for her uneasiness. The cabin was quite comfortable even though it was a bit spartan for a luxury yacht, and there was a new scent in its atmosphere too—the pungent, nose-tingling smell of Turkish tobacco.

'I am glad that you approve,' he said quietly, and the hint of sarcasm almost had her retorting defensively. But once again she bit her lip instead, and would not be drawn.

She looked around her at the wide, comfortable-looking bunk and the small table on which lay a battered copy of a familiar book, rather surprisingly in English. She walked over and picked it up, turning it to look at the title. *The Wind in the Willows*— she had not seen it since childhood, and she smiled instinctively.

'One of my favourites!' she said.

As she smiled she also turned and looked at him again and surprised a quite unexpected look in his eyes that she could not quite interpret, but which sent her heart lurching wildly for a moment until she regained control of her senses. It would never do to let herself be too attracted to her subject, not in this particular case, but each time she saw Celik Demaril she found something more about him that was disturbing to her emotions.

'How—how soon do we sail?' she asked in a voice that was not quite steady.

'In about ten minutes!' He sounded brusque and businesslike. 'Now if you will excuse me, Miss Palmer, I would ask you to stay here until we are under way, then I shall require you on deck.'

It was a strange way to word a request, if indeed that was what it was meant to be, and those disturbing doubts raised their heads again as she looked up at him with wide, wary blue eyes. 'What—what about the others?' she ventured. 'I mean the other people who are coming.'

The blue eyes fixed themselves on her steadily, and she could have sworn there was a glitter of malice in their depths. 'Everyone else is aboard,' he told her quietly.

'Oh, I see!' She blinked uneasily, shaking her head. 'It's just that I thought——'

His short tcch of impatience cut her short. 'I hope you will co-operate, Miss Palmer,' he said coolly. 'Otherwise——' A broad-shouldered shrug spelled out the rest of the message and she hastened to re-assure him. She was too near her goal now to risk upsetting him and have him put her ashore at the last minute.

'Yes, yes, of course,' she said. 'I'll stay here until we're under way, and then come on deck, yes?'

He inclined his dark head briefly, then stepped backwards into the narrow passageway and closed the door behind him. Seconds later she heard the soft swishing sound of his rope-soled shoes as he presumably went back towards the companionway.

Standing in the middle of the cabin, she clasped her hands together and smiled as she put them to her mouth, then spread her arms wide and danced a couple of short steps around the carpeted floor. Now she was aboard, and that was more than half the battle won, no matter what happened from here on. It would be difficult for him to evade her for very long in the restricted confines of a vessel at sea, and she regretted only that Kadri could not have come too and taken a picture record of her triumph.

It was rather less than ten minutes before she heard the deep, throbbing pulse of the engines surge into life, and she shivered with anticipation to think that at last she was about to achieve her goal. The request, almost an order, to present herself on deck as soon as they were under way probably meant that she was to be given the interview right away, and she was nothing loath to have it that way. After all, once she had it safely written down he could do nothing about changing his mind again.

She watched from the porthole as the shimmering turquoise sea swished gently with their progress, and would have liked to go on deck and wave goodbye to Kadri, for he would almost certainly still be there. But with her host's injunction in mind, she stayed where she was.

She stayed at the porthole for several minutes, watching the sun-bright sea and the glimpse of the Bey mountains to one side of the bay, hazy with heat and deceptively soft and dreamy-looking. It was some time before she realised that she would soon be expected on deck, and she ran a smoothing hand over her dress and her hair before she walked over to the door.

Cautiously opening the door a few inches, she put her head out and looked along towards the companionway. There were two other doors besides her own, but neither of them were open or even ajar, nor was there any sign of anyone else about, and that, once again, struck her as odd.

Even if guests were expected to stay below until the procedure of leaving harbour was safely accomplished, there should surely be some sign of life by now. She could hear voices on deck, but none of the light, carefree chatter she would have expected, and there was no laughter, no sign of the girls she had anticipated would be aboard to enliven Celik Demaril's trip.

All the voices she could distinguish were definitely male and she stopped suddenly, a cold sense of foreboding curling in her stomach. Her heart was hammering in alarm and she hesitated even about leaving the cabin, let alone going on deck, standing there with her hands clutching the edge of the door frame with her teeth biting hard into her lower lip as she looked along the passageway with anxious eyes.

Footsteps on the companionway sent another cold shiver along her spine, especially when she recognised them as belonging to Celik Demaril, and she gave a small gasp as she swiftly ducked back into the cabin and leaned against the door, her eyes wide and anxious.

'Miss Palmer!' Hard knuckles rapped sharply on the door and she bit her lip so hard she almost drew blood, her heart surging wildly in her breast as she tried to think of some excuse not to leave her cabin.

Those gory stories of pirates and slavery that

Kadri had regaled her with last night would not leave her, and she was shaking like a leaf, despite the fact that she knew she was being quite idiotic.

'I'm—I'm not feeling very well,' she called out in a strangely hoarse voice. 'Please—I don't want to come out!'

There was silence for a minute, so that she almost thought she had convinced him, but then the voice spoke close to the thin wooden partition and she almost jumped out of her skin in alarm. 'I cannot believe that you are so quickly suffering from *mal de mer* on a dead calm sea,' Celik Demaril told her calmly, 'and I do not know what you hope to achieve by such a pretence, Miss Palmer. You will please come on deck at once.'

'No!'

He said nothing, but she could imagine easily enough that black frown, and the glittering anger in those blue eyes because she defied him. A moment later the handle of the door turned and she realised for the first time that there was no way of locking it.

Her weight against it was of little use, and it took him only a moment to push her aside and come into the cabin, his height dwindling the polished ceiling to claustrophobic proportions. Standing just inside the door, he looked down at her, his blue eyes more amused than angry, and that in itself surprised her.

'What is the reason for this sudden—shyness?' he asked in a quiet, almost lazy voice, and Linsie shook her head.

'I—I'm not shy,' she denied. 'I—I just don't feel

92

like coming *on deck.*'

'I see.' He stood for a moment looking down at her, and Linsie had never felt so unsure of herself in her life before. The blue eyes swept slowly over her from head to toe in a way that brought that swift curling sensation to her stomach again. 'You do not appear to be suffering in any way,' he said.

'I—I don't—I mean I——'

'You had no hesitation in accepting my invitation,' he reminded her quietly, 'and you took great pains to be on the quay in time, fearing I should go without you, so you said. Why do you now behave as if I have kidnapped you against your will?'

Linsie shook her head. It was too difficult to find the right words to tell him of her suspicions and her forehead was already unpleasantly damp from the stifling heat in the cabin. 'I—I don't mean to behave like that,' she told him, brushing her tongue swiftly over her dry lips. 'Of course I don't think you've kidnapped me.'

The blue eyes were watching her closely, and she found it hard not to meet them. It was almost as if he knew exactly what was going on at the back of her mind. All those silly stories about Side——

'Has your—companion been trying to persuade you not to come?' he asked softly, and she would like to have objected about that brief but telling pause before he mentioned Kadri.

'He didn't want me to come,' she agreed.

'But you would not be persuaded, of course!'

Linsie flushed, ready to defend herself, whatever

93

the circumstances. 'I have a job to do,' she reminded him. 'And I mean to get what I came for.'

'Ah yes, to discover how I spend my leisure time, hmm?'

There was something in the way he said it, in the depth of those blue eyes that trickled a warning along her spine and made her shiver once again. 'Millionaires' parties, the things they do and say, are of interest to people,' she told him, wishing her voice was not so hoarse and husky-sounding. 'Most people would never know what it was like aboard a yacht like this if they didn't read about it in magazines.'

'And you mean to tell them?'

'I mean to try,' she said. She looked up at him, seeking some clue, some reassurance from those blue eyes but finding none. 'I—I can't hear anyone else about,' she said. 'I—I expected more people. '

'Women?' he asked softly, his wide mouth curled slightly into the mockery of a smile. 'You expected a horde of young girls? Is that what you had in mind to regale your readers with, Miss Palmer?'

Linsie hastily averted her eyes, and did her best to look as if nothing had been further from her mind. 'Not necessarily,' she denied, but his short, hard laugh showed how far he believed that to be true.

'I am sorry to disappoint you, Miss Palmer,' he told her shortly. 'But I take my sailing seriously, and a horde of young women would not be helpful in the least in the efficient running of my boat.'

'I—I didn't only mean girls,' Linsie protested, suddenly even more uncertain that she had done the right thing in coming. At least a party of young girls would have given her a better sense of security than she had at the moment. 'I just thought there would be more people, friends perhaps, a small party enjoying a cruise.'

One dark brow expressed surprise, although she felt certain he had been perfectly well aware of what she expected. 'Did I say anything to lead you to suppose there would be a—party on board? he asked in a soft voice, and his blue eyes glittered down at her darkly. 'There are the members of my crew and myself aboard, that is all, and yourself, of course.'

Linsie stared at him, her lips parted, her eyes wide and unbelieving. 'Only—you mean I'm the only—oh no!'

'There are no other women aboard,' he confirmed calmly, 'but surely, Miss Palmer, you are accustomed to such arrangement in your—free society?'

Linsie could think only of Kadri now, back there on the harbour, probably still watching the big gleaming yacht draw away, out into the turquoise sea, wondering how she was going to fare. If only he knew how she had been misled, surely he could do something to help her.

'I—want to go on deck,' she said, licking her dry lips once again. 'I want to see——'

'Your Turkish friend?' he asked softly, and she saw the faint quirk of his mouth at one corner that made him look cruel. 'I think he would take it that your anxious waves from the deck were merely gestures of farewell, Miss Palmer.'

Linsie swallowed hard, seeing the logic of what he said. 'I—I want to go back!' she demanded in a small, quavery voice, but he was shaking his head, even before she had the words out of her mouth.

'I think you know that is impossible,' he told her quietly, and again that long, cruel mouth tilted into a smile that gleamed in his blue eyes.

'But—' She felt horribly close to tears, and anger churned inside her at the idea of being so easily fooled, making her even more inclined to cry like a baby in sheer frustration. 'You—you can't take me against my will,' she told him huskily. 'You can't— it isn't legal!'

'Against your will?' He was leaning against the panelled wall of the cabin, his weight resting on one extended arm, and it was obvious to Linsie that he was enjoying every minute of it. 'That would have been possible four hundred years ago when this was a slave route, but now——' One large hand spread out in a gesture of denial. 'You came of your own free will, Miss Palmer, after going to unbelievable lengths to interview me.'

'But I didn't know—' she started to object, only to be waved to silence by that same big hand.

'Even your—friend will vouch for the fact that you came of your own free will,' he insisted in the same cool, quiet voice. 'Did you not immediately drive down to the harbour because I might possibly go without you? That was what you said, I think.'

It was all so indisputable, Linsie thought bitterly. She had been lulled into a sense of false security,

96

ignoring her own feelings of doubt, so determined to have that interview that she was prepared to go to almost any lengths, and now she was trapped here on his yacht, unable to turn to Kadri for help, or to anyone else, for it was unlikely that any of his crew would help her.

It was what he had in mind for her that worried her most at the moment, and she looked at him anxiously through the thickness of her eyelashes. 'If you don't intend to give me the interview,' she ventured huskily, 'I don't see why——'

'You may write what you will when we return from Side,' he interrupted quietly. 'You will have little time on the trip, I think.'

Again Linsie started at him unbelievingly, her mouth parted and her eyes wide. 'I—I don't know what you mean,' she whispered.

He tipped back his dark head and looked at her down the length of his arrogant nose, the blue eyes gleaming in the dim stuffiness of the cabin. 'I carry no passengers, Miss Palmer,' he told her softly. 'You are a member of the crew as far as I am concerned—therefore you will be expected to do your share of the work on board.'

'You——'

He merely swept that disconcerting gaze over her again, and nodded his head. 'You look strong and healthy,' he said with satisfaction. 'The work will do you no harm!'

CHAPTER SIX

By refusing to leave her cabin Linsie felt she was taking the only action possible. If Celik Demaril expected her to knuckle down to the same discipline as the members of his crew, he was going to find her far less amenable than he evidently expected.

It was now nearly twelve o'clock, midday, almost two and a half hours since they left Antalya, and the cabin was becoming unbearably hot. There appeared to be no air-conditioning of any sort and it was obvious that very soon she would have to seek the comparative coolness of the deck or stifle in the heat.

She had tried opening the portholes, but the brass screws fastening them proved too difficult for her to turn and she had finally given up and stretched herself out on the bunk, her forehead already beaded with perspiration.

It was a little after twelve-thirty when she realised that the aroma of cooking food was permeating even the confines of the cabin, and she sat up on the bunk and sniffed appreciatively. Even the heat could not diminsh her always healthy appetite, and the delicate scent of *çerkez tavugu* was unmistakable even at a distance. Her mouth watered for the taste of tender boiled chicken, walnuts and red pepper, and she could resist it no longer.

Getting to her feet, she padded softly across to the door and opened it just a crack, listening. The only sounds appeared to be coming from on deck, and somewhere a man laughed, perhaps happily anticipating his meal. Encouraged, Linsie put her head round the edge of the door and peered out cautiously. There seemed to be no one about, but the sudden access to fresher air after the stifling confines of the cabin made her close her eyes in momentary bliss.

'Miss Palmer!'

He must have come from the door almost opposite during the seconds she had her eyes shut, and he was looking at her with the same unrelenting look he had left her with when she refused to go on deck. It was too late to duck back inside, and anyway, the air in the cabin was by now almost unbreatheable. Instead she stepped out into the narrow passage and closed the door behind her.

'It's unbearably hot in there,' she said, as if she had every right to complain about her accommodation, and he nodded.

'The air-conditioning is switched off,' he told her.

'It isn't working?' Linsie asked, and saw the deep gleam of malicious laughter in his eyes.

'It will work when you do, Miss Palmer,' he said quietly.

For a moment Linsie stared at him in disbelief, then she shook her head slowly. 'You wouldn't,' she said huskily. 'Even you wouldn't do anything so—so despicable!'

'The choice was yours, *hanim*,' he told her coolly. 'I do not carry passengers, as I told you. I gave you passage on my boat so that you could see first hand just what it was like and write your—whatever it is, accordingly. It is surely not asking too much that in

99

return you do a few minor tasks on board.'

Linsie was eyeing him warily, almost willing to allow him to persuade her if the return was not too great. 'Just what,' she asked, 'am I expected to do?'

'I do not expect you to carry out work beyond your capabilities,' he said. 'But I know that young women in your country often become crew members on boats of this kind.'

'From choice!' Linsie retorted swiftly. 'I didn't sign on as a—a deckhand, I came as a guest—at your invitation!'

'You accepted my invitation to accompany me on this trip,' he reminded her quietly. 'I did not specify that you would be treated as a guest.'

His tall powerful frame completely blocked the narrow passage and for a moment she experienced a brief thrill of fear when she looked up into that strong, dark face. Here in the cool dimness below deck, he looked much darker altogether.

His skin, his hair, even the blue eyes looked almost black in the shadows, and she shivered involuntarily. He looked completely Turkish and quite ruthless, and Kadri's stories of pirates and slavery came pouring back into her mind again as she looked at him.

'I—I misunderstood,' she admitted, curling her fingers tightly in an effort to retain what courage she had left. 'I wouldn't have come if I'd realised what— what I was expected to do.'

'Oh, I think you would!' Those expressive brows passed comment, doubting her. 'I understood that you were prepared to go to any lengths to obtain your

100

story, Miss Palmer. You will surely not be deterred by the prospect of cleaning the deck of my yacht!'

Linsie was staring at him, blank-eyed with disbelief. 'You—you're telling me that you—you expect me to go swabbing decks like a deckhand?' she said hoarsely. 'You can't be serious!'

'Oh, come now,' he remonstrated in a soft, reasonable voice, 'it is surely much less arduous than walking all the way up the hill road to Farik in a hot and heavy disguise!'

She was shaking her head, half believing that the heat had somehow affected her brain, that she was imagining all this, but there was nothing imaginary about the tall, very real man in front of her. 'You're doing this for—for revenge,' she whispered, still not quite believing it. 'You're doing it purely and simply to pay me back for invading your precious privacy!'

For a breathless moment Linsie wondered what he would do when he took a half step towards her, and she put her left hand to her throat in an instinctive gesture of defence. In fact he did no more than stand for a moment, looking down at her, but there was a tense, vibrant virility about him that was like an assault on her senses, and the warmth of his nearness sent a strange tingling sensation through her whole being.

'I admit that it gives me some satisfaction to have you in this situation,' he admitted after a moment or two. 'But you cannot complain now that you have achieved your object. You sought my company against my will, *hanim*, and now you have no choice but to bear it for as long as you are aboard my yacht. How—unpleasant you find your trip must depend on yourself.' For a moment only, the dark face broke into a gleaming white smile and the blue eyes glittered with laughter as he shook his head at her. 'I am sure most of your readers would enjoy such a situation, *hanim*, why not you?'

'You—you can't expect me to enjoy being treated like—like one of your men,' Linsie objected breathlessly, and he shook his head once more, a brief, telling glance at her slender shape only adding to her discomfort.

'I would not give up my cabin for one of my men,' he told her coolly. 'You are already privileged, Miss Palmer, do not expect further privileges.'

Linsie swallowed hard on the latest revelation, although it scarcely came as a complete surprise. There were several signs that should have told her who the cabin belonged to. Its masculine, almost spartan air and that lingering scent of Turkish tobacco—only that English copy of *The Wind in the Willows* struck an alien chord, and she made a mental note of that as something to be investigated.

'I didn't realise the cabin was yours,' she said. 'It wasn't necessary for you to turn out of it on my account.'

One dark brow flicked briefly upwards. 'You would have preferred to share the crew's quarters?' he suggested softly, and Linsie shook her head.

'No, of course not, but——'

'Please do not concern yourself,' he begged, as if

102

she was doing just that. 'I have the cabin of the first officer—it is almost as comfortable. I do not expect you to suffer hardship, *hanim*.'

'You expect me to scrub decks!' she insisted. 'That's not woman's work!'

'It most certainly is,' Celik Demaril argued calmly. 'But scrubbing will not be necessary, however, a mop is all that is required. And even you, *hanim*, I think, know how to use a mop and bucket—it is far less strenuous than your earlier endeavours to interview me.'

'You won't let me forget that, will you?' she asked bitterly, regretting still further her unsuccessful venture as a Turkish washerwoman.

'You made it difficult for me to forget it, Miss Palmer,' he told her coolly. 'I suspect every person who comes into my home since you gave me cause.'

'But I—' A large hand silenced her with an imperious gesture, and she obeyed its injunction without hesitation.

'You may return to your cabin or report on deck,' he told her shortly. 'I am going to eat my meal.'

He would have turned and left her, but Linsie reached out instinctively and touched his arm, hastily withdrawing her hand when her fingers came into contact with the firm, golden smoothness of his skin. 'I'm—I'm hungry too,' she said in a small and rather breathless-sounding voice. 'You surely don't mean to starve me, do you?'

There was an unconscious look of appeal in her wide blue eyes and her mouth had a soft, tremulous look when she thought of being deprived of food on top of all the other indignities she was expected to suffer for the sake of getting that precious interview. For a moment she feared her appeal was to be dismissed out of hand, but then he shook his head slowly.

'It depends upon you,' he told her in a quietly reasonable voice. 'Sometimes hunger is a great spur to work.'

'If I *don't* eat,' Linsie retorted desperately, 'I won't be able to work at all—willingly or not!'

'You are right!' he nodded coolly, as if the logic of it appealed to him. 'Starving you is not practicable.'

'Thank you!' Her sarcasm fell on stony ground, but it gave her a certain amount of satisfaction. 'Do I eat with the crew?'

He apparently took her question quite seriously because he considered it for a moment before he answered, and his obvious lack of preparation led her to realise that he genuinely had not expected her to accompany him on the trip.

'I think not,' he decided at last. 'They would not welcome the presence of a woman and I do not wish there to be trouble among my crew.'

'Then where *do* I eat?' Linsie asked. She was beginning to feel quite tearful at the thought of that delicious food she could smell, and none of it coming her way so far. 'Have you a cell?' she suggested bitterly. 'Perhaps I should be put in irons for—for mutiny or something!'

'Perhaps you should!'

He eyed her narrowly for a moment, then indicated with a brief nod that she should follow him. He opened the door nearest the companionway and stood back to allow her through first, but she hesitated, his last words in mind. It was not a cell, however, but a small dining salon with a shiny wood table and two chairs set at either side, with another at its head.

The table was laid for only one, so it was obvious that he had anticipated eating alone, and she stopped to wonder what impulse had made him invite her to join him when he was so obviously bent on making her as uncomfortable as possible.

The room, though quite small, was blessedly cool and it was evident that here at least the air-conditioning was working. It was wood-panelled, like the cabin she occupied, a pleasant little room, titillatingly full of the most delicious smells, and she already felt a little better as he saw her seated before taking his own place at the head of the table.

Evidently even in her precarious position she was to be treated with a certain amount of courtesy, and she thanked heaven that his manners owed more to civilisation than those dark, craggy features did. She was aware, however, that in such close proximity she found him even more disturbing, and it troubled her.

The large, strong hands and powerful-looking arms, the deep golden darkness of a glimpse of broad chest where the white shirt opened—there were so many things about him that she found herself noticing, and she had never in her life before been so aware of a man, of his sensuality and the sheer essential maleness of him, and she almost sighed her relief aloud when a young man in a white jacket came in, presumably a steward.

Dark eyes noted her presence with startled surprise, and he murmured hasty words in Turkish to Celik Demaril. What explanation his employer gave, or even if he gave any, Linsie had no idea, but the young steward departed swiftly and returned with the necessary cutlery for another setting. He glanced at her curiously from the corners of his eyes as he placed each item carefully, and gave her a white-toothed smile of appreciation before he straightened up.

Celik Demaril, to Linsie's surprise, spoke to him sharply in his own tongue, and the young man disappeared hastily through the rear door again. It was almost as if he took exception to his steward making his admiration of her so obvious, and it gave her a strange sense of excitement for a moment.

'Hassan has—a certain reputation,' he said in his quiet voice as the young man departed. 'It is not often that he has such temptation put in his way while he is at sea.'

'Temptation?' Linsie looked at him a little vaguely. Her senses had been so violently responding to his own more potent attractions that she had hardly noticed the young steward.

Celik Demaril's blue eyes held hers steadily for a moment, then slowly moved over her features, as if to encompass every detail of them—the pale softness of her skin and the full mouth slightly parted as she looked at him curiously with deep blue eyes, the small nose and long fair hair.

'You are very lovely,' he said quietly and matter-of-factly. 'Surely you have no false modesty about your looks, Linsie Hanim.'

Linsie's heart fluttered uneasily, and she tried to steady its beat by putting both hands in front of her on the edge of the table and then leaning forward so that they pressed to her breast. 'I—I try not to be coy about it,' she admitted in a voice that sounded, to her own ears, quite dismayingly small and shaky.

His using the Turkish form of address sounded so much more intimate than the formal 'Miss Palmer' he more usually called her, although she knew that it was purely her imagination that made it seem so. The compliment, too, had been meant as no more than a factual comment, she felt sure, even though it had caused such havoc to her senses.

'You do not then need my warning about Hassan?' he suggested, and Linsie shook her head.

'Not really,' she said, but could not resist putting a wealth of meaning into her voice when she looked at him. 'However, forewarned is forearmed, Mr. Demaril, and it's always useful to have advance information on just what a man has in mind for you.'

Whatever he would have replied was left unsaid when the impressionable Hassan returned with their meal, and Linsie thought it was probably as well that she had not had the opportunity of making further rash jibes like that.

She could deal with Hassan's type easily enough, should the need arise, but Celik Demaril was another matter altogether. She had no desire to become involved in another argument with him, or to arouse his anger—particularly not before she had eaten.

The *çerkez avugu* was excellent and Linsie did justice to it, unaware that her host was regarding her appetite with a kind of surprised tolerance that would have amazed her had she noticed it. Only when she had disposed of the last morsel of chicken and made sure that no crumb of ground walnut remained did he remark on her obvious enjoyment.

'You like Turkish food?' he asked, and she nodded. She felt somehow more confident now that she was no longer hungry, and more comfortably cool.

'Most of it,' she agreed. 'Selim Bey's wife is a very good cook, and we eat very well there.'

He poured wine into both their glasses, a luxury she accepted gratefully, then leaned forward on his elbows, inhaling the bouquet of the wine from the glass held in both hands. 'Do you cook, *hanim*?' he asked.

Linsie regretted the return to a more formal term of address, but she nodded her head and smiled as she raised her glass to her lips. 'As a matter of fact I do,' she said, and flicked him a look that was frankly provocative. 'Did you expect me not to?' she challenged, and saw the swift bright glitter that came into his eyes.

'In a society that allows its women such—liberties,'

he told her coldly, 'one does not know what to expect of them.'

Linsie looked down at the sparkle of wine in her glass, then tipped the glass slightly so that the diffused sunlight from outside caught the rich colour of the liquid and made it shimmer with life. She did not look at him as she spoke. 'And you don't believe in liberty?' she suggested softly.

He was shaking his head and a brief, wary glance betrayed a hint of smile at the corners of his wide mouth, as if he suspected her of trying to draw him into more serious dispute. 'I believe there is a limit to the freedom a woman should have,' he stated quietly. 'Once over certain limits her pleas become battle cries and she becomes less of a woman, and much less attractive. Men do not cherish their opponents.'

Linsie felt a strangely lilting sensation in her heart as she listened to him, although she was far from convinced by his argument. 'And Turkish men cherish their women?' she asked softly.

His dark head came up swiftly, as if he suspected sarcasm, but she was still studying the sparkling liquid in her glass and she did not look up. 'It is our way,' he said.

'I see.' Sitting there with her eyes downcast to the glass she held in her hands, she might have been accepting his views quite meekly, but she looked up suddenly and there was a bright gleam of challenge in her eyes. 'You're very adamant in your views, Mr. Demaril,' she told him in a small but insistent voice, 'and yet you have no conscience about keeping a woman aboard your yacht against her will, the only woman among heaven knows how many men.'

The blue eyes met hers squarely, a glitter in their depths that could have been laughter or anger, it was impossible to tell which. 'Oh, you have nothing to fear, *hanim*,' he told her quietly. 'My men will not touch you.'

Her heart was racing wildly and she felt quite light-headed with some inexplicable emotion that was probably deepened by the potency of the wine she had consumed, and she looked at him still with that challenge in her eyes.

'And do you exclude yourself from the—men?' she asked softly.

The jibe went home, she saw that from the sudden tightening of his mouth and the way the strong fingers curled more firmly round the stem of his glass. She had been unforgivably rude, she knew it; as she knew she would not be allowed to get away with it.

'The situation is of your choosing, *hanim*,' he said coldly. 'The customs of your country allow such situations and I cannot change the opinions of foreign visitors to my country.' The blue eyes glittered at her almost blackly in that dark, craggy face and she felt the cold shiver of fear like the touch of ice on her skin. 'As for your last question, *hanim*,' he told her harshly, 'if yellow hair and pale skins were to my liking I would show you soon enough whether or not I may consider myself a man!'

Linsie almost stifled with the strong, hard beat of her heart and she could have wept to see such compromise as had been achieved during their lunch together destroyed by one rash statement that she had been unable to resist. Her hands were trembling as they held the almost empty wine glass.

'I—I didn't mean to imply——'

'I am not a fool,' he interrupted harshly. 'You meant to anger me and you have succeeded, Miss Palmer. One assumes that your desire for revenge has now been satisfied.'

'But please let me——'

'You have said enough!' He stood up, towering over her, and his big hands were so tightly clenched that Linsie feared they might at any moment hit out. Swiftly she got to her feet and stood beside him, her heart beating anxiously. 'I must remind you that you are required to act as a member of my crew,' he added coldly. 'Mustafa will tell you what is required of you when you go on deck.'

Linsie felt very close to tears and she wished that Kadri was near to comfort her. It was possible that tears were one way to solve the present situation, for surely nothing would be considered more feminine, but somehow she felt that her stock had already sunk too low with Celik Demaril for it to work for her.

She had to pass him to get to the door and she shrank even from doing that, for he looked like some huge dark figure of vengeance standing there. Then she shook her head and moved across the room, brushing by him as she went, not saying a word in case those threatening tears made her look a complete fool.

In the doorway she hesitated, wanting to try just once more to explain how impulsively she had acted. Turning her head, she looked at him over one shoulder, her mouth parted and tremulous as she sought for words.

'If you—if you could——'

She stopped when he moved, fearful of his intention, but he neither said nor did anything for a moment, simply looking down at her with that disturbing glitter in his eyes again. 'You still doubt me,' he said in a fierce, soft voice.

His hands, hard and strong on her upper arms, pulled her into his arms, pressing her close against the fierce hardness of his body, and she looked up into those blue eyes for only a second before he bent his head and kissed her—a kiss that made her senses swim, despite its lack of gentleness, a fierce attack on her emotions that left her with no strength to struggle or breath to cry out, and she felt herself go limp against him, helpless as a child.

When he released her she stood for a second with her eyes still closed, then those violent hands slid from her arms and she looked up at him. For a moment he looked down at her narrow-eyed, then he shook his head and moved away from her to stand by the table, turning after a moment, one hand to the thick brown hair at the back of his head.

'I have no doubt that you are not unfamiliar with this situation,' he said in a cool, matter-of-fact voice that brought a flush of colour to Linsie's cheeks. 'I had not meant it to occur, however, and I am sorry that it has.'

Linsie stared at him, scarcely able to believe that he was not apologising to her but simply stating regret on his own behalf. 'You—you think I'm used to being treated like that?' she asked in a husky whisper. 'You think I take such things in my stride?'

For a moment he looked at her curiously then he narrowed his eyes again. 'You have surely been kissed before,' he said with certainty, and Linsie flushed, unable to deny it. But how to make him understand that this was something quite different from a brief snatched kiss after a party or a dance, was seemingly impossible.

'You—you wouldn't understand,' she said in a small, husky voice. 'You just wouldn't understand.'

One dark brow kicked upwards and he looked at her steadily for a moment, then briefly, that hint of smile touched his mouth again and the blue eyes had a deep, glowing look. 'Oh, I think I do, *hanim*,' he told her softly. 'It is you, I think, who does not understand.'

CHAPTER SEVEN

LINSIE, in cotton trousers and a tee-shirt, reported on deck to Mustafa, the first officer, and found him to be the elderly man she had seen first when she came aboard. He proved to be a kindly man and it was evident that the experience of having a woman, and particularly a European woman, among his crew was not only new to him but something he did not altogether approve of.

She was startled to discover when she first came on deck just how far they had travelled, for Antalya had disappeared into the hazy distance. Mustafa, in passing, noticed her looking across the water at a town sitting hazily on the distant coast, and informed her that it was Side.

'Side?' She looked startled. 'But I thought——' She gazed at the passing coastline and shook her head, all those previous misgivings returning.

Mustafa looked at her enquiringly, his lined face softened by a curious gentleness. 'You are surprised, *hanim*?' he asked softly, and she nodded.

'I though Side was as far as we were going,' she told him. 'I didn't realise how close it was to Antalya.'

'It is only a very short distance, *hanim*,' he told her, anxious that she should not be alarmed. 'Did you not expect to be aboard for two days or more?'

'Oh yes, yes, I did, of course.' She still watched the ancient beauties of Side gleaming warmly in the haze of heat off their port bow, and felt a small uneasiness. 'I—it was just that I thought it was further away, that's all,' she explained. 'I thought it would take longer to get to Side itself.'

'Not very long,' said Mustafa, still with that curious and soothing gentleness. 'I think that Alanya is

114

our destination, *hanim*—a place of much beauty.'

'I'm sure it is,' Linsie agreed with an absent smile. Something in his reply had puzzled her. 'But don't you *know* our destination, Mustafa Bey?' she asked. 'Surely in your position——'

The old man's shoulders shrugged lightly and there was a hint of smile in his narrowed eyes. 'I am not the master of the vessel, *hanim*,' he reminded her softly. 'I take orders from Celik Bey. There are times when we call at Side, but today Celik Bey has said that we go on, and it will surely be Alanya, I think, So——' He shrugged again, and at that moment Celik Demaril himself came on deck, and any further conversation was curtailed for the moment.

She worked at a leisurely pace with her mop and stayed in what little shade the deck offered as far as possible, but even so she was obliged to spent most of the time in the hot, bright sun.

Her chores, in fact, proved far less arduous than she had expected, and no one made any comment on the leisurely pace at which she worked, certainly not Mustafa, who watched her with more concern than censure. It was he who gravely advised her to cover her head, and his obvious concern for her welfare made her see him as a valuable ally, despite the fact that he was obviously loyal to his employer.

Before very long she had to admit that she was beginning to enjoy the experience. It was bright and sunny on deck, much more pleasant than being in that stuffy cabin, and there was also a pleasantly light wind that cooled her and led her to believe that the

115

sun was less fierce than it actually was.

With Mustafa as an ally she admitted to feeling happier about her position, for the old man, she felt sure, would not allow any harm to come to her, and the knowledge allowed her to relax a little and make the most of what was, after all, a quite novel experience, and would surely read well into her feature on Celik Demaril.

The change of destination, she could see, had been a possibility from the beginning, for she had expected the trip to last for two or three days and there was no reason, at the moment, to suppose it would be any longer, if Mustafa was to be believed.

The two younger members of the deck crew seemed to view her addition to their ranks with more curiosity than disapproval, and it was evident that the novelty of it was something they would talk about when they returned home. Nor would they step out of line, despite their frequent and speculative glances—not with Mustafa's eagle eye on them.

Celik Demaril scarcely appeared on deck at all during the afternoon and Linsie wondered whether he was busy on some below-deck activity, or whether he was deliberately staying out of sight, perhaps bothered by some belated quirk of conscience.

An invitation to join him in the little salon for dinner was not altogether unexpected, although it had crossed her mind during the afternoon to wonder if she would be expected to eat in her cabin—thus remaining as unobtrusive as possible. She was tired, but quite pleasantly so, after her unaccustomed activity, and she flopped straight down on her bunk, her feet curled up under her when she came below, so that the knock on her cabin door with the invitation to dinner had her frowning curiously.

The message was delivered by the dark-eyed Hassan, and he made his appreciation of her fairness even more blatantly obvious now that he did not have the sharp eye of his employer to deter him.

Hassan, Linsie thought, was the only member of the crew likely to chance the wrath of Celik Demaril by attempting to flirt with her, and somehow the idea intrigued her. Not that she thought for one moment that he was jealous of his young steward, of course, but he had spoken pretty sharply to him at lunch when Hassan had dared to show admiration in those expressive eyes of his.

It was only when she washed and changed into a dress, ready for dinner, that Linsie realised how the warm wind on deck had tricked her into thinking that the sun was less fierce than it was. Her arms, where they had been exposed to the sun by the short-sleeved shirt, felt quite stiff and painful, and already had a hot, angry look that threatened further discomfort.

Slipping the soft coolness of white lawn over her head, she discovered that her neck and shoulders had also caught too much sun, and she pulled a face at the angry redness that marred her fair skin. If she had been seeking a reason for making Celik Demaril relieve her of her duties on deck, she had an excellent one.

Another point she noted was that the air-conditioning in her cabin had been restored, as Celik Demaril had intimated it would be when she agreed to do as he said. Not that it wasn't still rather too stuffy for her, but the portholes remained immovable. Perhaps, she mused, Hassan would open them for her if she asked him.

'*Hanim*?' A gentle tap on her cabin door brought her swiftly from the realms of speculation and she hurried across to open the door, '*Aksam yemegi, hanim*,' Hassan informed her with a wide, approving smile for the sleeveless white dress.

Linsie did nothing to encourage the look in his eyes, but looked at him curiously. 'Dinner?' she asked, and he nodded, his perfect white teeth gleaming in the darkness of his face.

'*Evet, hanim*,' he replied, which obviously meant yes, if that bobbing head was any guide, and Linsie glanced back into her cabin before following him. She would have liked to put some sunburn cream on her arms at least, but she was wary of keeping Celik Demaril waiting.

It would not really have surprised her to find her host wearing evening dress, even in these circumstances, but she was relieved to see that he wasn't. A jacket had been added to the cream shirt and trousers that could have been the same ones he wore to lunch, and he turned from looking out of one of the portholes as she came in, the blue eyes sweeping swiftly and boldly over her.

She had thought that angry kiss forgotten, or at

least put to the back of her mind with things best forgotten, but the sight of him revived the same disturbing emotions she had tried so hard to stifle, and she found her heart was beating much faster than it should have been, especially under that all-embracing gaze.

'I—I wasn't sure what I should wear,' she said, looking down at the flimsy brevity of the white lawn dress.

It clung lovingly to the soft curves of her body as far as the waist, then fell in soft folds that showed off her slim legs, its paleness giving her an ethereal look that even sunburned arms could not spoil.

There had been little time to do much with her hair, but she had brushed it until it shone, then left it loose about her shoulders, partly because it helped to hide the red soreness of her neck and shoulders. She wished she had taken similar precautions with her bare arms, but it was too late now and he was already frowning over the fiery red marks on her fair skin.

'You are burned,' he said, ignoring the invitation to comment on her dress. 'I did not notice that your arms were not covered when you were on deck.'

'Would it have made any difference?' Linsie enquired softly, and for a moment he looked at her steadily without answering.

'I have no wish to see you hurt,' he told her quietly, at last. 'You will be well advised to wear something with long sleeves when you go on deck again.'

'I haven't anything.' His look, she thought, accused

her of being difficult. 'I haven't anything with long sleeves,' she explained. 'I wasn't expecting to spend several hours on deck working in the sun, you see, I didn't come prepared. If you had warned me——'

'*Touché!*' The soft-voiced surrender made her blink uncertainly for a moment and her heart leapt uneasily when a definite smile softened the craggy features for a moment. 'But no matter what you think, Linsie Hanim, I did not intend that you should be harmed in any way.'

'I—I know.' She did not look at him again, but strove to do something about that way her senses were reacting to that smile. She did not remember ever seeing him really smile before and the effect of it was quite devastating.

'Come,' he said, 'let us have our dinner.' He saw her seated as he had at lunch, and she felt a curling sensation in her stomach when he leaned over her to push in her chair, his sleeve brushing her bare arm. 'Mustafa tells me that you have worked well,' he told her as he took his own seat, and Linsie cast him a brief but telling look through the thickness of her lashes.

'Mustafa is a very nice man,' she said. 'He's very kind and understanding.'

The blue eyes glittered with amusement at the jibe when she had expected resentment. 'Mustafa has many sons,' he said quietly. 'He would have liked a daughter—also he does not approve of me putting you to work. In fact, Miss Palmer, you have made conquests of three of the men aboard.'

'Three?'

Linsie looked up swiftly, her eyes searching the dark face for some clue to the identity of the third man. She could safely count Mutafa as a conquest, she thought, and of course the impressionable Hassan, but the third one she did not dare gues at.

Celik Demaril's blue eyes glittered at her from below arched brows, and that hint of laughter was still in their depths, only now it mocked her. 'Kemal, one of the deck hands, is apparently quite impressed both with your beauty and your courage,' he explained, and added softly, 'Who else had you in mind, *hanim*?'

Linsie, her heart tapping anxiously at her ribs, refused to be drawn, and yet again she had cause to be grateful for Hassan's sudden appearance with their meal. The fare was not exotic, but there was plenty of it and it was excellent when one considered that it must have been prepared in the confines of the yacht's galley.

A man like Celik Demaril, of course, would expect to live well, even when he was at sea, and she was probably underestimating the size and scope of the galley, but all the same she had been pleasantly surprised with the meals she had had so far.

Succulent baked lamb stuffed with *pilâv* rice was followed by a salad and then a dessert which was quite new to her and which her host described as *asure*. It turned out to be a kind of boiled pudding made of some kind of cereal with figs and hazelnuts, and was quite delicious.

121

She took her coffee *az serkeli*, since she found the heavily sweetened brew favoured by most Turks far too sickly, and once more Celik Demaril observed her enjoyment with apparent satisfaction.

They sat for quite a long time over dinner, although conversation was no more than spasmodic, and she wondered at the tranquillity of their silence. It was seldom that she found it easy to sit quietly with another person and still feel at ease, and it was strange that she could do so with this man of all people.

'You will put on something soothing?' he said, when she at last rose to go, and one long finger gently touched her sunburned arm.

Her pulses leapt in response to his touch and she nodded. 'I meant to before I came in to dinner,' she told him a little breathlessly. 'But I didn't want to keep you waiting.'

Standing beside her, he reached out and brushed the long hair aside from her neck. 'Your neck and shoulders too,' he said. 'Can you do that yourself?'

'I—I expect so.' It was disturbing the way every nerve in her body reacted to the gentleness of those strong hands, and she felt suddenly and wildly elated, although she strove to subdue the feeling as idiotic. 'I haven't much choice, have I?' she added, trying to sound practical. 'There's no doctor or nurse aboard, or even another woman.'

For a moment he hesitated, and she could feel the tautness of will power that held him in check, then he opened the door of the salon for her and inclined his head as she passed him in the doorway. 'I hope

122

you do not experience too much discomfort, *hanim*,'
he said in an unnaturally stilted voice.

Linsie half turned as she crossed the narrow passageway. 'Tomorrow—' she began, and he looked
down at her steadily.

'Tomorrow,' he said softly, 'we will be in Alanya.'

Linsie had smoothed on sunburn cream so that her
arms felt a little less burningly uncomfortable, but
her neck and especially her shoulders were less easy
to treat, and she had had to leave them as they were.

Even the coolness of soft sheets did nothing to
alleviate the discomfort and she got up again after a
few minutes and walked restlessly across to the
nearer porthole, wishing she had remembered to ask
Hassan to open it for her. It was not dark outside
for a full yellow moon sat like a beatific Eastern god
in the purple sky and the usually turquoise sea glim-
mered and shone in shades of midnight blue and
black with every ripple, gold-topped by the moon.

It was tempting to go on deck, but that would mean
dressing again, and that was too much trouble. Instead she stood by the porthole gazing out at the sea
and the sky and feeling rather dreamily romantic
about the setting. As a background for some exotic
romance it was perfect, but nothing was further from
reality as far as Linsie was concerned at the moment.

She was in the act of piling her long hair loosely
on top of her head in an attempt to ease the burning
sensation on her shoulders when she almost started
out of her skin and stared at the door unbelievingly.

Not quite believing she had heard that faint tap, she listened with her heart beating so hard she could hear nothing else but its clamour.

Then she heard it again, and for a moment stood there in the moonlit cabin with a hand to her mouth, her eyes wide and half afraid in the dusk. If it was simply Hassan trying his luck, she would soon deal with him, but she had a strangely certain feeling that it wasn't Hassan.

Her bare feet padded soundlessly across the carpeted floor and she opened the door swiftly, her eyes drawn to the broad back just disappearing into the cabin opposite. He turned and she met the uncertainty of his gaze with some surprise. For Celik Demaril to look uncertain about anything was unusual enough to make her stare.

He did not speak for a moment but stood looking at her, his eyes staying resolutely on her face instead of straying to the revealing firmness of her robe. 'I am sorry if I woke you,' he said, his voice low and slightly husky, as if he was unsure what to say next.

'I wasn't asleep.' For the first time since she had met him she felt she had the upper hand, and it gave her a strange sense of power as she looked up at the strong dark features even more strongly drawn in the soft light of the passage.

He had removed his jacket and his arms were bare, strong and powerful-looking like the big hands that slid uneasily into his pockets. 'I had thought to help you with your sunburn,' he said, still sounding oddly stilted and unnatural. 'You cannot do anything about

124

your shoulders, I think.'

'I can't,' she agreed, the overhead light casting dark shadows where her long lashes hid her eyes. 'But you really shouldn't have troubled, Mr. Demaril.'

For a moment he almost smiled, and she felt her heart respond, swiftly and urgently, to it. 'Since I am to blame in some part for your being burned,' he said softly, 'I should perhaps contribute to easing the pain.'

'Thank you.'

He looked at her for a moment, not quite certain if he understood, she thought, then he cast a swift glance at the open door of his cabin and stepped across to join her, his tall figure completely blocking the doorway.

The warmth of him enveloped her like an embrace and she stepped back into her own cabin, her eyes wide and fluttering uncertain. He did not put on the light, and she was reminded that he knew his way about this cabin better than she did, a realisation that only added to her uncertainty.

'The cream, Linsie Hanim,' he said softly, and she reached for the jar beside the lamp on the small table that occupied the centre of the room.

The door was still open and she spent only a moment wondering for whose benefit that precaution had been taken, then she felt the gentle touch of strong fingers as they slid the soft robe from her shoulders. 'I will try not to hurt you,' he told her softly.

125

There was no sound but the vibrant throb of the engines as they slowed down ready to stop and drop anchor for the night, and that huge moon still lent its yellow light to the little cabin. Linsie stood with her hands holding the neck of her robe together, high under her chin so that the back of it draped down below her shoulders and exposed the fair, sunburned skin.

His touch was unbelievably gentle for such a man, and she felt herself shivering inwardly at the sensation it created, sliding over her shoulders and soothing in the cream. She closed her eyes and thanked heaven that he had not needed to put on the light, for she had never in her life been so affected by a man, and somehow it must show.

'That is easier?' He asked the question in that same quiet voice, and she nodded, unable to speak at the moment, while he slid the robe back into place.

'Thank you.'

There seemed little else to say, and she was stunned by her own reaction, putting her hands to the tops of her arms and looking up at him in the shadowy light from the passage.

'Tomorrow,' he said, 'you will take more care.'

'I'll try.' Her voice sounded small and she tried hard to steady it. 'There's not much I can do without sleeves to cover my arms and a higher neck.'

He studied her for a moment, then shook his head slowly, as if he anticipated her answer even before he spoke. 'I suppose you would not consider wearing one of my shirts?' he suggested, and Linsie stared.

126

'Your—one of your shirts?' she echoed. 'But——'

'It would be better protection for you, if you have nothing of your own with sleeves,' he insisted. 'And it would cover the back of your neck too.'

For a moment she considered the idea, then suddenly felt like laughing, though for no good reason she could think of. 'All right,' she said, and smiled up at him. 'Why not?'

She thought she caught a brief glimpse of that smile again, but could not be sure. 'Why not?' he echoed softly. 'I will see to it that you have one in the morning, *hanim.*'

'Linsie,' she said, rashly lightheaded. 'Why do you have to be so formal?'

It was not the right thing to say to him, she thought, as soon as the words had left her lips. His upbringing had endowed him with a curious mixture of manners and customs, but mostly he followed his father's beliefs, and her attempt to take the initiative would sound much more bold and unfeminine to him than it would have done to someone more used to European ways.

The blue eyes, darker in the diffused light from the passage, looked down at her for a moment, then he nodded, still looking quite serious. 'Goodnight, Linsie,' he said softly, and this time there was no mistaking the smile as it gleamed briefly in the shadowy darkness of his face.

Only the benevolent moon witnessed the startled way she blinked at him in stunned disbelief as she murmured a subdued goodnight, watching that broad back disappear through the door, abruptly shutting out the light. How, she wondered hazily, did this particular man manage to create such havoc simply by using her christian name and smiling as he said it?

Half expecting a different situation in the broad light of day, Linsie would not have been surprised if she had been relegated to a solitary breakfast in her cabin, but the invitation to join Celik Demaril in the salon came via the dark-eyed Hassan, as usual.

Their meal was the customary Turkish breakfast of tea in a tall glass, taken with *simits*, those circular breakfast rolls, and jam, butter and cheese. They ate it in almost silence, and Linsie thought her companion was more than a little preoccupied, although she would not have dreamed of suggesting it.

It was when she was about to leave the salon, after her meal that he called to her over one shoulder, where he stood looking out of one of the portholes at the smooth glitter of the sea. It was more than ever obvious that he had something on his mind, and she felt a curious curling sensation in her stomach as she speculated on what it could be.

He put a long flat Turkish cigarette between his lips and for a moment the bright little flare of the lighter flame lent added depths to his craggy features. 'It would be better if you did not spent so much time in the sun today,' he said at last, and Linsie shook her head.

'Do I have any choice?' she asked quietly. 'If I am

to work, as you expect me to, I have to be in the sun for a good deal of the time.'

A swirl of blue smoke concealed the expression on his face for several moments, and he still did not look at her. 'It will not be necessary for you to continue with your—your——'

'Chores?' Linsie suggested softly, not quite believing she could be hearing aright, and he looked at her at last, a sharp-eyed, narrow look, as if he suspected her of sarcasm.

'It is obvious that you cannot be expected to expose yourself to the risk of serious sunburn,' he said quietly. 'Therefore you may do as you please, *hanim*, I will not extract conditions from you.'

Linsie gave it some thought, her mind whirling off into all kinds of fascinating speculation. Something had made him change his mind, soften even, and she found it hard to believe that it had simply been the sight of her burnt shoulders and arms last night. Celik Demaril, she decided, was an enigma, but a dangerously fascinating one.

'Will I still get my interview?' she asked softly, and for a moment he held her gaze, his eyes narrowed behind the screen of blue smoke.

'Tonight we will be in Alanya,' he said quietly. 'There will be much for you to see, many things I can show you that you can write about.' Again the blue eyes watched her as he spoke. 'Have you not been to Alanya?' he asked, and she shook her head.

'Never,' she confessed.

The deep, quiet voice had an almost hypnotic effect

on her senses and she felt no wish to be anywhere else at the moment, except standing there in the little salon, listening to it. It was a strangely tranquil sensation—as if it was not quite real.

'There are many things to be seen in Alanya that cannot be seen elsewhere,' he told her. 'And the view is breathtaking.'

Linsie smiled. 'You speak with native pride,' she suggested softly, and he nodded.

'Possibly more than you realise,' he agreed. 'I was born in Alanya—it is my native town.'

It seemed to Linsie that a new note of intimacy had been introduced into the conversation, and it did not even occur to her at the moment that he might be simply attempting to provide background for the feature she was to write about him.

'This coast is beautiful, as you can see,' he said. He was once more looking through the porthole and he indicated the hazily distant shoreline with one hand. 'But nowhere is it more beautiful than Alanya. There are endless coves, coloured grottoes such as you have never seen before.'

'It sounds wonderful,' said Linsie, gently prompting, for she wanted nothing so much at the moment as to prolong this odd sense of tranquillity. 'It must be very exciting.'

'Enchanting,' Celik Bey said softly, his gaze still on that distant shoreline. 'It is an enchantment that few places offer, and I think you will enjoy it.'

'I'm sure I will,' she agreed, strangely touched by his feeling for the place of his birth. 'I—I wish you'd tell me more about it—about the colours and the—grottoes.'

'What can I tell you?' he asked. 'There are so many things—natural beauties with romantic names. The Lovers' Grotto, the Blue and Green Grottoes, there are so many. Not all of them romantic in your eyes, perhaps, but interesting to the student of history.' For a moment he turned and looked at her. The blue eyes had a bright glitter in their depths, like laughter. 'There is also Kizlar Magarasi, the Maidens' Grotto,' he said softly, 'but perhaps I should not show that to you, it would offend your—sensibilities.'

Linsie blinked at him uncertainly, not sure if that laughter was meant to mock her or invite her to share his amusement. 'How could it do that?' she asked, and he did not at once reply, but drew deeply on the cigarette, his head back to exhale the smoke from his lips slowly.

'This was once a coast much frequented by pirates,' he said. 'Kizlar Magarasi is where they kept their fairest captives—it was their harem!'

'Oh, I see.' She refused to look even slightly shocked, but glanced at him from the thickness of her lashes. 'And you approve of such practices?' she asked softly.

He shook his head slowly, but there was still a hint of laughter in his eyes as he looked at her. 'Had I lived in those times I have no doubt I would have done my share of pillaging and plundering,' he said, 'and also taken my share of the harem, but—' He shrugged his broad shoulders, and Linsie felt again that irresistible aura of fascination that seemed to emanate from him.

'Shall I write that about you?' she asked, and he smiled. 'You may write about me as you find me, Linsie Hanim,' he said quietly.

Linsie shook her head slowly and looked at him with a small, speculative smile, wondering if it was possible for anyone to get close enough to a man like Celik Demaril to really know him. 'I'm grateful to have been released from my chores,' she told him, 'and I look forward to seeing Alanya. I'll—I'll do my best to write about you as I find you—but it won't be very easy.'

The blue eyes held hers steadily, narrowed against the spiralling smoke. 'No one finds me easy, Linsie Hanim,' he said softly.

CHAPTER EIGHT

WEARING one of Celik Demaril's shirts and her own cotton trousers, Linsie looked and felt rather like a street urchin, especially with her long fair hair pushed back under the small-brimmed denim hat she wore to protect her from the sun. Mustafa viewed her garb with a mixture of doubt and approval. He obviously thought she should have more protection from the sun, but he was doubtful if she should have been wearing clothes belonging to his employer. For herself, she felt very comfortable, and did not mind in the least that the borrowed garment was much too big for her.

It was shortly after breakfast the following morning, while she was leaning on the rail, looking across at the dragon's-teeth rocks that guarded Alanya's sandy coast and the thrusting prominence of the Red Tower at the entrance of the old town, that she felt someone watching her.

Drawn by the intensity of the watching eyes, she turned and saw Celik Demaril standing just behind her, his own lean frame similarly clad to her own. White trousers and the twin to her own borrowed shirt combined to make him appear even more dark than usual, and she felt that curious and disturbing curling sensation in her stomach again when she looked at him.

'You are not going ashore in my shirt?' he asked softly, but in such a way that it was as much a statement as a question, and Linsie shook her head.

'Oh no,' she agreed smilingly, 'I can hardly walk about on shore looking like this!'

She was aware, not for the first time, of Mustafa's benevolent eye on them and wondered what construction the old seaman put upon her being there. He could scarcely have missed the initial antagonism that had existed between herself and his employer, and he must surely find their present rather wary truce cause for even more speculation.

Celik's eyes ran over her slowly, a lurking gleam in their depths that stirred strange and disturbing emotions in her. The white shirt she wore was made less voluminous by the addition of a makeshift belt in the form of a coloured scarf tied round her waist, and the sleeves were rolled to above her elbows, but even so the shoulder seams still came well down her arms and the neck gaped, despite the fact that she had turned up the collar at the back to protect her neck.

It reached to below her knees too and under that slow, expressive scrutiny she felt small and vulnerable, but at the same time oddly elated too. 'It would be as well if you wear something a little more conventional,' he agreed quietly. 'Although for some inexplicable reason you look almost more feminine wearing my shirt than you do in a dress.' Briefly the white teeth showed in the darkness of his face, betraying a smile. 'It is a strange contradiction, is it not?'

Linsie had not, until now, felt at all self-conscious about it, but suddenly the improvised belt about her waist seemed to emphasise its slimness and exaggerate the soft curves above and below it.

She smoothed trembling hands up over the thin material where it covered her collarbones and drew the collar of the shirt up higher round her neck in a curiously defensive gesture. Holding the collar points at either side of her face, she looked up at him, her elbows close together in front of her.

'Not really so strange,' she said huskily. 'English women have been following fashion and wearing men's shirts for some years now—for much the same

134

reason.'

'I see—it is all part of this search for freedom that you want? This wearing of men's clothes?'

Linsie shook her head, praying it was possible to answer him without starting up another disagreement. She looked at him through her lashes, seeking the right words. 'I think in a way it's quite the contrary,' she told him. 'As you said yourself, Mr. Damaril, a woman can look more feminine in man's clothes than she does in her own.'

'Hmm!' He came and leaned against the rail close to her, regarding her still with that same steady and disconcerting gaze, a hint of smile just touching his mouth. Then he swept that all-embracing gaze over her again. 'The result is not always so pleasant, I think,' he said softly, and Linsie curled her fingers swiftly into her palms.

She sought another subject, one less personal and less disturbing to her self-possession. Pointing across the water, she shaded her eyes against the sun. 'That's Alanya, isn't it?' she asked, and he nodded.

'That is Alanya,' he agreed quietly. He too looked across the sparkling water to the impressive and inspiring height of the town on the rock high above the sea, then he spoke without turning his head. 'Mustafa will accompany us while we are ashore,' he said, and added swiftly, as if some explanation was needed, 'for your protection.'

She had nothing at all against Mustafa, but Linsie was not at all enamoured of the idea of having him as a chaperone, and her frown expressed as much. For *my* protection?' she asked.

'Of course,' Celik agreed quietly. 'It would not be for mine, *hanim.*'

She frowned too, over his formality. Less than forty-eight hours ago he had smilingly, and apparently willingly, called her Linsie when she had asked him to, but since he had reverted to the more formal manner, and she wondered if he regretted that moment of intimacy.

'Linsie,' she prompted softly.

For a moment the blue eyes scrutinised her steadily, then he shook his head, as if something was beyond his comprehension. 'You invite such familiarities,' he said. 'Do you not fear for your—your safety?'

'No.' She shrugged, feeling both defensive and uneasy, as if he had criticised her for being promiscuous. 'I've never had cause to regret being friendly, I see no reason why I should now.'

The bright sunlight gave his eyes a fierce depth, and lent shadowy harshness to those craggy features so that for a moment she wondered if she was indeed taking risks with this man—risks that she had never even thought about before.

'You trust me?' he asked softly, and she nodded, almost without realising she was doing it.

'Yes, I trust you,' she said, and he shook his head again, as if such trust was beyond his understanding.

He regarded her for a long, nerve-shaking minute, then nodded suddenly, and it was clear that he had made up his mind about something. 'Very well,' he said quietly. 'Mustafa may go his own way and visit his son and his grandchildren. I shall be going ashore in about twenty minutes, if you will be ready by then, I will escort you.'

'You—you haven't anything to do—I mean,' she added hastily, 'you haven't any business in Alanya?'

He shrugged his broad shoulders. 'I sail for pleasure, Linsie Hanim,' he told her. 'I shall find pleasure in showing you the treasures of Alanya while we are here.'

Linsie looked up at him for a moment, her eyes shadowed by the brim of her hat, but still unusually bright and wide, hinting at mischief and excitement. 'And you won't mind being seen alone with me?' she asked.

For a moment his mouth was touched briefly by a smile and there was a deep, glowing look in his eyes as he regarded her steadily. 'Oh, I think I will be safe with you, Linsie Hanim,' he said softly.

Alanya was everything that Celik Demaril had claimed for it, and the view from the summit of the rock on which it was built was indeed breathtaking. The town itself was an enchanting mixture of religions and histories—its ancient walls owing their existence to the work of several centuries.

Christian and Muslim existed side by side, for some of the very earliest Christians had lived and died within its protection, and there seemed nothing incongruous about finding the slim minaret of a mosque and its attendant golden dome sharing the hot Mediterranean with a beautiful Byzantine church.

Having climbed some rather scary wooden steps to the very summit of the rock on which the town was built, Alanya looked like sheer enchantment, and not for anything would Linsie have missed it. The outline of the promontory itself seen against the turquoise sea with the jagged guard of rocks marching along the edge of the waves was like a slightly bizarre dream and she enjoyed it all immensely.

Celik Demaril proved to be an excellent, if slightly biassed guide, and Linsie had never seen him so animated as when he was pointing out the many spectacular sights of his home town. Near the ancient castle mulberry trees were growing, specially cultivated for the breeding of silkworms, the weaving of silk scarves being a main local industry.

The young girls offering the exquisite, multi-coloured silk scarves for sale were as irresistible as their wares, and a recognised feature of Alanya. The bright, beautiful colours of the scarves and the sheer luxury of the silk was a lure that Linsie found difficult to resist, but she shook her head more by instinct than for lack of desire to own one, when Celik offered to buy one for her.

The sensation she felt when he made the offer was almost like panic, and yet she told herself she was quite idiotic to see it as such. The girl selling the scarves flicked her dark eyes curiously between them, and once again Linsie felt curiously vulnerable just being with him.

Despite his lighter than usual colouring and his blue eyes, it must have been obvious to the girl that the man was Turkish, and it just as obviously intrigued her to see him in the company of a golden-haired and fair-skinned European. Intrigued her enough to make her speculate.

'Do you not want to have one?' Celik asked, frowning over Linsie's shaking head, and she instantly denied it.

'Oh, of course I do,' she told him frankly. 'I'd love one, but—well, it wouldn't be right.'

'Right?' he questioned her use of the word, and one dark brow expressed surprise as well as dislike of standing in a public place debating the right and wrong of buying a scarf for her. 'You cannot mean that it is not ethical,' he told her in a cool voice. 'Or is this refusal to accept gifts some strange quirk in your code that I am unaware of, Linsie Hanim?'

'It isn't a quirk at all,' Linsie denied, aware of those dark eyes watching them with renewed interest now that there was tension between them. 'It's just that——' She shrugged suddenly and looked up at him with a small, wry smile. 'I suppose it doesn't really make sense in this day and age,' she admitted.

'Not in your world, surely, *hanim*,' he said softly, then indicated the waiting scarf seller with a jerk of his head. 'Choose which one you prefer,' he said. 'It will serve to protect your shoulders from the sun.'

The incredible softness of the silk had a seductive feel in her fingers, and Linsie held two of the scarves in her hands, unable to decide between them. Both

139

were exquisite, both tempting in their way, and no doubt expensive too. She would never, in normal circumstances, have allowed a man she had known for such a short time to buy her anything so expensive, but somehow the usual standards seemed not to apply where Celik Demaril was concerned.

It was while she was still trying to decide that Celik suddenly took some coins from his pocket and handed them to the smiling girl, who bobbed her head in appreciation of the double sale. 'Keep them both,' he told Linsie with a hint of smile for her surprise. 'And lie about their purchaser, if the truth should prove embarrassing.'

Catching the brief, provocative glance he gave her when he made the suggestion, Linsie felt the colour in her cheeks and looked up at him sharply. 'Why should I need to lie?' she demanded, and he shrugged his broad shoulders carelessly.

'How would I know that, Linsie Hanim?' he asked softly, and took her arm, leading her away from the curious dark eyes of the girl with the scarves. 'Please put one of them round your shoulders,' he added. 'You are too exposed to the sun.'

She nodded, willing enough to wear her newly acquired finery, and a moment later they stopped to enable her to do as he suggested. They stood close against a rough red stone wall in a niche formed by the junction of two walls, and it seemed to Linsie that there was no one else about suddenly, just the two of them in the small, secret niche of red stone.

To thank him too profusely for the gift, she felt,

would embarrass him, but she looked up and smiled as she ran the soft silk through her hands. 'Thank you,' she said softly.

Now that they had stopped walking she was aware of a new and uncomfortable sensation of dizziness that had nothing to do with the warm vibrancy of him sharing the niche in the wall, but her fingers were not quite steady as she slid one of the scarves about her shoulders—so unsteady that she dropped one end of it and made a grab at it as it slipped through her fingers.

Her own attempt failed, but Celik retrieved it swiftly and drew the sensual softness of the silk up over her bare shoulders. As he reached round her his body was pressed close to hers, the sweep of his arm drawing her close, encircling her as he reached for the end of the scarf and raised it to cover her fair skin.

A warm, spicy maleness enveloped her with heart-stopping suddenness and she felt her heart clamouring loudly while his long fingers tied the silk in a loose knot, just above the curving neck of her dress. Again she was assailed by that strange sense of isolation, as if there was no one but the two of them in the whole world, but the trembling of her legs she recognised as attributable to something else besides her reaction to him, and they felt so weak she almost fell.

'Is that comfortable?' His voice was soft, much more soft and deep than she had ever heard it before, she would have sworn, and she nodded, licking her dry lips before she could speak.

'Yes. Yes, thank you.'

'Linsie?' He did not move off as she expected him to do, but instead put one arm across her as if to protect her, and there was a faint hint of a frown between his brows. 'You are not feeling faint, are you?' he asked. 'You look——' One large, expressive hand expressed concern as well as another meaning. 'Perhaps you have already been in the sun too long.'

'No, no, really I'm fine!' She could not face the embarrassment of being taken ill in such a public place, but she was not averse to his display of concern for her. She laughed, a little uncertainly. 'I'm just a bit—a bit lightheaded, that's all.'

'Lightheaded?' He looked puzzled, and she smiled.

'A bit like being drunk,' she explained. 'Only I'm not drunk on alcohol, but on your beautiful scenery.'

'Ah, I see!'

The explanation seemed to please him, although she was sure he was not entirely convinced by her explanation. She was beginning to see her imminent collapse as inevitable, for her head was aching with a heavy dullness that nauseated her, and she felt less and less like walking on her dangerously unsteady legs.

'There is one thing I'd like to do,' she said, seeking an excuse to leave the busy street for something quieter. 'I'd like to phone Kadri, if it's at all possible, and let him know where I am.'

'Your Turkish friend?' he asked, and curled his lip in much the same way he had before when he

142

spoke the same words, so that she wondered what it was about his compatriot that he disliked.

'Kadri is Turkish, certainly,' she said quietly, determined not to have him belittled. 'So are you, Mr. Demaril, and I can't think why you're always so—so disparaging when I mention him.'

For a moment she thought he was going to be angry, and she was finding it difficult enough to act sensibly as it was without having to cope with his anger as well. Instead, however, he merely shrugged and there was a small half smile on his mouth as he looked at her.

'I have never met your friend,' he said quietly. 'I have no reason to like or dislike him, but it is obvious that you like him quite a lot or you would not so swiftly fly to his defence.'

Linsie put a hand to her throbbing head and sought for explanations, and it did not even occur to her that he had absolutely no right to an explanation of any sort in the circumstances. 'I like Kadri,' she told him. 'I'm—I'm under his protection in a way—at least, I'm under his father's protection, and at the moment, while we're on this job, Kadri is standing in for his father.'

The blue eyes had a bright, glittery look as if he suspected much more than she had told him and did not approve of any of it. 'To be under such protection——' he began, but Linsie interrupted him quickly and without stopping to care whether or not he took kindly to the interruption.

'Mr Lemiz senior and my own father are friends

143

of long standing,' she informed him. 'While I am in Turkey the Lemiz family are mine, in a manner of speaking. Kadri's like a—a brother to me.'

He said nothing for a moment and Linsie tried hard not to let him see how ill she felt. Her head was throbbing more violently than ever and she felt dismayingly sick suddenly. 'Then you must let me help you call him on the telephone,' he said quietly at last. 'If you would like me to, of course.'

Linsie managed a smile. 'I would, thank you,' she said in a small husky voice. 'My Turkish is practically non-existent.'

They found a telephone in a convenient *gazino* and, after he had obtained the number of the hotel for her, Celik left her to make her call while he sought the refreshment of coffee. Selim Bey answered and apologised most profusely for Kadri Bey's absence; he had gone out, he informed her.

'Gone out?'

She felt quite unreasonably cross with Kadri for not being there, but realised that her mood was due to her feeling so terrible. Her brain refused to work, and she could think of nothing but contacting Kadri, letting him know where she was, although he was probably not expecting to hear from her until Celik's yacht returned to Antalya.

'I am sorry, *hanim*,' Selim Bey said, evidently taking her present silence for disapproval. 'There was word, I think, that the boat of Celik Bey was seen going towards Alanya. I think that Kadri Bey has taken the motor car to see for himself, *hanim*.'

144

Linsie's head was spinning wildly and in the stuffy heat of the telephone kiosk she found it even harder to stay conscious. 'It—it doesn't matter,' she said, in a tight little voice. 'If—if he comes back——'

She managed to get no further, for the little kiosk suddenly began to spin round and round violently, and the telephone became too heavy for her to hold. She had a fleeting vision of a man's face looking startled as he passed by the kiosk, and then there was nothing more.

'Linsie! Linsie!' The voice was oddly familiar, and yet it was not the one she expected to hear, and Linsie frowned as she opened her eyes, closing them again instantly when the light hurt them.

Hands held hers tightly and reassuringly and the voice was again calling her name, trying to rouse her from the swaying unreality of semi-consciousness. 'Linsie, please wake up!'

'Kadri?' She turned her throbbing head and tried to focus on the familiar good-looking face, but registered only the eyes, bright, dark and angry as well as anxious, and anger was something new to the Kadri she knew.

He touched her face lightly and then bent his head to look at her more closely, his hands again holding tightly to hers. 'What has he done to you?' he asked in a voice so harsh with anger that she scarcely recognised it as his.

His fingers brushed lightly, almost caressingly, over her sunburned arms, the bright patches of red on her fair skin, and on her shoulders. 'You are burned by the sun,' Kadri went on accusingly. 'And you were lying there in that kiosk unconscious when I saw you—what has he done to you?'

She appeared to be in a small room of some sort, lying on a kind of settee, and the buzz of voices that had been so noticeable in the *gazino* were now no more than a distant hum, so presumably she had been moved from the café itself.

There was some special reason, she thought hazily, why she must not make an exhibition of herself by fainting in public, and the softness of silk, crumpled under her shoulders, reminded her suddenly. Trying desperately to concentrate, she turned her head again.

'Celik?' She looked up at the other two faces that hovered above her, but both of them were unfamiliar and she frowned anxiously. 'Celik,' she said again. 'Where is he?'

It was plain that Kadri found her concern not only puzzling but distasteful, and he frowned, something that she had seldom seen him do before, and certainly never so blackly. 'He has gone back to his yacht,' he told her shortly.

'Without me?' It seemed such a silly thing to worry about when she felt so awful, but she hated to think of him abandoning her when she most needed him, and despite Kadri being there she felt that Celik Demaril would have given her more the reassurance she needed.

Kadri's frown deepened. 'He did not like hearing the truth about himself in public,' he told her, and

146

the satisfaction with which he said it made it obvious that he had been the one who publicly berated Celik Demaril.

Even in her present state Linsie could well imagine the effect of such a scene on him and she felt desperately like crying suddenly. Great shiny tears squeezed between her half-closed lids and rolled down her cheeks and she shook her aching head from side to side despairingly.

'Oh no, Kadri!' she whispered. 'No, you didn't!'

'I was worried about you, Linsie.' He spoke softly, and she could imagine that he did not relish the idea of the other two watchers being a witness to his confession. 'I perhaps spoke more angrily than I would have done, but when I saw you there——'

'I—I felt faint,' Linsie said in a small unsteady voice. 'But it—it wasn't his fault—it wasn't anyone's fault, I just——'

'Don't talk now,' Kadri advised. 'A doctor is coming to see you and then I will take you back with me.'

'A doctor?' Her throbbing head tried to cope with the idea of a doctor being called to attend her. 'I don't need a doctor, Kadri, I——'

'You will please lie there quietly until he arrives,' Kadri instructed firmly, and she had neither the strength nor the inclination to argue with him.

CHAPTER NINE

LINSIE felt very much better, and Selim Bey's wife had contributed a great deal towards her recovery. She was a round-faced, cheerful woman, remarkably pretty for her age, and frankly missing her daughter, now a practising doctor and living away from home. She spoke a little English, but was in no way as fluent as her husband, and she had confessed to a desire to have been in the same profession as her daughter in her younger days.

Selim Bey himself had proved a good host, and Linsie had wanted for nothing during her illness. Sunstroke was not new to him, he told her, and he would see that she was well cared for.

Only one thing troubled her during her recovery, and that was the thought of Celik Demaril. He was constantly on her mind, and it was such a new sensation to her to have a man so persistently in her thoughts that she was uneasy about it.

He had been furiously angry when he left the little *gazino* in Alanya, according to Kadri, but he had offered no denial of his responsibility, and Kadri had taken that as evidence that he was to blame, no matter how much Linsie denied it. Seemingly he had simply allowed Kadri to take responsibility for her and returned to the yacht, angry but too proud to offer explanations.

What troubled Linsie most was the fact that he had not attempted to see her or communicate with her since and, sitting on the secluded privacy of Selim Bey's balcony, she contemplated her own future actions, as well as speculating on her erstwhile host's.

It was true that the now faded sunburn had been Celik's fault basically, but he was nothing like the villain that Kadri tried to make him, and he had made amends immediately, even taking the unorthodox step of coming to her cabin to render assistance.

After that things had been different and, although their truce had at times been rather a wary one, she had enjoyed the rest of her time in his company and was ready to admit it. Seeing the sights of Alanya with him had been more exciting than anything she had ever dreamed of, and she would have been the first to admit that the person of her guide had contributed as much, or more, to her enjoyment as the place itself.

Now—she shook her head as she leaned it back against the cushions, protected from the sun by an overhanging roof. Now it was almost back to the beginning again as far as she and Celik Demaril were concerned, thanks to Kadri, and she bit hard on her lower lip at the thought of never seeing him again.

Boy-friends had come and gone in her young life, but their departures had never affected her with any more than a faint tinge of regret. Celik Demaril, she admitted, was very different. He was a mature and sophisticated man, difficult to forget, and one who had made a greater impact on her than any man had ever done before.

She had only to close her eyes, as she did now, and

149

that dark, craggy face was before her, with its wide, expressive mouth and blue eyes, the thick brown hair sweeping across half the broad brow. Shaking her head to dismiss the illusion, she got to her feet, suddenly restless. Celik Demaril was well out of her reach, and would have been even if she had not been a journalist.

Kadri welcomed her appearance and, seeing him, she could not find it in her heart to condemn him too harshly, for he had been swift and fierce in her defence, and surely no woman could ask more of a man, no matter how misguided his defence had been.

His dark eyes missed nothing of the shadows that still lingered under her eyes, nor the pale fairness of her skin after several days out of the sun. He took her hand as she came towards him, and that too troubled her to a certain extent.

Kadri had always treated her with a rather touching old-world politeness, anxious about her at times, at other times impatient with her schemes or resigned to them, but since her return from Alanya there had been subtle differences in his manner.

Before, he had never indulged in actual physical contact, whereas now he seemed to have no such reticence. He took her hands, lightly touched her cheek or took her arm as she walked, and the difference, while small, was noticeable and significant. Kadri would never have allowed himself such familiarities unless his own attitude towards her had changed, and he thought he had the right to them.

She had made as little as possible of her initial

shock of finding herself the only woman aboard the yacht, when she told him about it, but his anger had been so frightening in its intensity that she had thought it best to gloss over her short spell as a deckhand, for fear of his reaction.

'You still look pale,' he said softly, when she appeared. 'Should you not still be resting, Linsie?'

'I'm fine now,' Linsie told him. 'In fact I thought I'd go out for a while.'

He looked worried, as she had guessed he would. 'Go out?' he echoed. 'But it is not wise, Linsie.'

'Oh, nonsense! I've only had a mild attack of sunstroke.' She laughed, but a gentle hand on his took away any suggstion of mockery for his concern. 'I'm perfectly all right, Kadri, honestly, and I really need to get out on my own for a bit. Everyone's been very good to me, but I'm beginning to feel—stifled, indoors all the time.'

Kadri's dark eyes speculated for a moment, then he shrugged resignedly. 'I cannot make you stay in,' he admitted. 'But do not do anything rash, I beg you, Linsie, and I must come with you.'

Afraid of appearing ungrateful as well as ungracious, she hesitated. 'I'd—I'd rather like to go alone,' she said.

'Oh!' He looked at her for a moment, then shook his head slowly. 'If it is what you wish,' he said in a somewhat cooler voice, 'there is nothing I can do, but——' He looked down at her, his eyes searching her face for some clue to her intention. 'Please promise me that you will not do anything foolish,' he

151

begged. 'The—the story, the feature on Celik Demaril, I know it was important to you, but——'

'It can still be written,' Linsie interrupted quietly. 'I have enough material to work from, and I can produce quite a good article with what I have—better than I'd hoped for.'

'You will not try to see him again?' He sounded anxious and she was surprised that her own reaction was impatience rather than appreciation of his anxiety.

'I doubt if I'll ever see him again,' she said quietly, and swallowed hard on a sudden lump in her throat. She looked up at Kadri's good-looking face and shook her head. 'But if I have the slightest opportunity,' she added, 'I *shall* see him, Kadri, because I want to.'

'Linsie!'

'Please, Kadri!' She put a gentle hand on his arm. 'I have a lot to think about, and I need to walk and be alone.' She covered her fair hair with the little denim hat and settled one of the silk scarves that Celik had bought her round her shoulders. 'Don't worry,' she told him softly, 'nothing can happen to me this time—I won't be gone very long.'

The sensation of freedom it gave her to be on her own again was pleasant, and Linsie meant to make the most of it. She liked Antalya and by now its streets were almost familiar to her, but still a source of pleasure.

Walking along one of the main streets, she was

shaded from the sun by a row of palm trees lining the banks of a natural stream. Such unexpected advantages as the surfacing of the many subterranean streams were used by the Turks to beautify their city, and their frequent appearances were part of Antalya's charm.

Linsie was not the only one to spend a few moments enjoying the sight and sound of the cool water as it rushed along between its banks of flowers, and the short, rough-barked palms that squatted like giant pineapples on either side. The pleasantness of cool water and shade had a soothing effect and she found herself not so restless as she had been when she set out, although Celik Demaril was still very much on her mind.

Remembering her promise to Kadri not to do anything rash or to stay out too long, she spent some time speculating on ways of getting to see Celik again, but eventually sighed for her own lack of initiative and decided to return to the hotel. At the moment it seemed an insoluble problem.

She had emerged from the shade of the trees and was about to cross the road when she stepped back hastily as a huge, black limousine came into view, chauffeur-driven and with a woman passenger in the back.

It took her a second or two to recognise the passenger, and in the very moment she did so the car drew up at the kerb and the rear window was wound down. A head appeared in the opening, elegantly hatted in cream silk straw, and the blue eyes that

153

looked at her from the shadow of its brim had a faintly anxious look.

'Miss Palmer.'

It was not necessary for her to raise that soft and gentle voice, for the car was stopped immediately beside Linsie, and she smiled instinctively. 'Good afternoon, Contessa Contini,' she said, and already her eyes were searching the dim, cool interior of the car for another, more familiar face. The Contessa was alone, however, and smiling at her.

'Will you not join me?' she asked, and to Linsie the invitation was irresistible, even though she hesitated before accepting.

'Thank you.' She slid on to the rich softness of leather upholstery and sighed grateful thanks for the luxury of air-conditioning.

'Are you quite recovered from your ordeal?' the Contessa asked as the car pulled away from the kerb again, and Linsie nodded.

'Yes, quite recovered, thank you.'

The Contessa's blue eyes studied her for a moment with kindly concern. 'You still look a little unwell,' she told her gently, and Linsie smiled assurance.

'I'm fine now,' she insisted. 'Really.'

Her own nervousness, she recognised, stemmed from the fact that she had no way of knowing just what Celik had told his mother about the incident, or how largely her own part in it had figured. If only she had known the older woman better she would have ventured to explain something of what had happened, as far as she knew it, but the Contessa was largely an unknown quantity to her, and she was sure only of the fact that Celik would scorn any effort on her part to get to him through his mother.

The hot, bright streets of Antalya purred beneath the wheels of the limousine and the two silent women in the back seat remained strangely tense, held apart by their lack of knowledge of one another. It was only when Linsie realised that they were heading in quite the wrong direction for the hotel that she spoke again.

'I—I was going back to my hotel,' she ventured, and the Contessa smiled understanding and nodded.

'I have promised that I will—how is it?—pick up my son at this time,' she told her. 'If you do not mind the delay, we will gladly take you to your hotel on our return.'

'Oh no, no, of course I don't mind in the least!'

Linsie's head was spinning, and her hands and legs felt quite ridiculously weak at the prospect of meeting him again. She had thought of nothing else for the past few days, it was true, but she had not expected anything like this to happen, so suddenly and so unexpectedly, and certainly not through the offices of the Contessa.

The gentle blue eyes were looking at her and the Contessa shook her head slowly, a strangely wistful expression on her face. 'I do not know the full story of what happened during the time you were with my son, Miss Palmer,' she said quietly. 'Celik is very—reticent about his personal affairs, but I do know that he has been most unhappy these past few days,

155

and I suspect that you are involved in some way. Oh, please do not think that I blame you,' she added hastily. 'But——' Expressive hands reminded Linsie of her son. 'My son is not a man of dark moods, and since his return from Alanya there has been something troubling him that he will not even confide to me.'

'I'm—I'm sorry.' There seemed so little else to say in the circumstances, and yet it was obvious that a mere apology would not suffice, not when the Contessa's concern was so genuine.

'You know what is troubling him?' she pressed. 'What is making him unhappy?'

It was difficult to find the right words, and Linsie was not even sure if she would know them when they came. 'I—I think perhaps Cel—Mr. Demaril is more angry than unhappy, Contessa,' she ventured at last, and the Contessa's fine brows rose enquiringly.

'Angry?' she queried.

Linsie nodded, her hands in her lap, wondering how much she should say; how much the older woman had been told. 'It—it was my fault in a way, I suppose,' she admitted. 'I was so keen to get that interview with him—Mr. Demaril, that I went further than I should have done to get it. He thought he would teach me a lesson, only I didn't see it until it was too late.'

'I do not understand.' It was obvious that so much, at least, he had not confided to his mother, and Linsie wondered just what he had told her about the trip.

'When he issued the invitation to go with him on his yacht,' she explained, 'I didn't even stop to think of anything but the fact that at last I would be able to write about him in his own environment, among his friends.' She glanced up and pulled a rueful face. 'I didn't realise I'd be alone—I mean the only woman aboard.'

The Contessa shook her head slowly. 'That was very wrong of Celik,' she said without hesitation. 'But he is very Turkish in his thirst for revenge and he would not stop to consider the harm he could do.'

'As it happened,' Linsie confessed frankly, 'it was much less of an ordeal than you might suppose and after—well, after the first day, we got along quite well, and I have absolutely no complaints about the way I was treated, either by Celik or his crew. In fact,' she smiled and shook her head, 'I enjoyed it, even swabbing the decks like a sailor.'

'*Dio mio!*' The Contessa looked shocked. 'You were actually made to——' She murmured other words in her mother tongue, all of the uncomplimentary to her son, Linsie felt sure. 'Has he taken leave of his senses?'

'Not really,' Linsie told her, smiling ruefully. 'It was meant to put me firmly in my place, and really I wasn't put to work for very long.'

'I should think not,' the Contessa said indignantly. '*Dio mio!* What kind of a man is my son?'

Linsie was still smiling, mostly at the memory of a small stuffy cabin and large, gentle hands soothing the burnt skin of her shoulders with a gentleness that was not only unexpected but infinitely disturbing. 'He's very kind,' she said softly. 'When I was sunburned from being on deck, he was—gentle and kind. And I had a wonderful time with him in Alanya.' She stroked the soft silk that encircled her shoulders. 'He bought me scarves to cover my shoulders,' she said, and the Contessa looked puzzled.

'Then why,' she asked, 'should he be angry—as you say?'

Linsie looked down at her hands again, once more seeking the right words to explain. 'It was because of Kadri,' she said.

'The young man I met at your hotel?' Linsie nodded. 'He is very good-looking, Miss Palmer.'

'He's a very good friend, Contessa,' Linsie countered. 'Kadri's family have taken me under their wing while I'm in Turkey, and at the moment Kadri is responsible for my wellbeing. He takes his role very seriously.'

'Of course,' the Contessa agreed. 'The Turks take their family role very seriously.'

'It was because Kadri thought—he thought Celik had ill-treated me,' Linsie explained. 'In fact I'd had too much sun and I would have said something before about feeling unwell, but I didn't want to spoil our tour of Alanya, and I insisted I was all right. Then——' She shrugged and tried to convey how she had felt in that stuffy little kiosk. 'I wanted to ring Kadri, and Celik got the number for me, then went to have a coffee. I collapsed and Kadri happened to be there—he'd come to Alanya to look for me and

158

I don't suppose we were all that hard to trace. He saw me before Celik—Mr. Demaril did.'

'I see.'

'Kadri was worried,' Linsie explained, 'or he would never have been so—so rude. He accused Mr. Demaril of—oh, heaven knows what! Anyway, Mr. Demaril had gone back to the yacht by the time I came round and I haven't seen him since.'

'This good-looking young man is—jealous?' the Contessa suggested delicately, and Linsie shook her head.

'Good heavens, no!' she denied hastily, but even as she said it she wondered if the Contessa wasn't right. Kadri was so very different since they came back from Alanya, she had noticed it herself, and his reaction to Celik's behaviour, imagined or otherwise, was typical of jealousy.

'Ah, so many misunderstandings!' The Contessa raised eloquent hands and shook her head.

'I—I wanted the chance to explain to Cel—Mr. Demaril,' Linsie told her, and the Contessa smiled faintly.

'Then it is well that I saw you, is it not?' she asked. 'Perhaps you will now have the chance to explain, Miss Palmer.'

'Do you think so?' Linsie asked, not very hopefully. 'I have an uneasy feeling, Contessa, that Celik is not a very good listener when it comes to explanations, and he probably isn't very interested.'

'Oh, *mia cara signorina*,' the Contessa scolded gently, one gloved hand covering hers. 'Have I not

159

said before? You do my son an injustice—he is not such a hard man as he sometimes appears. Have you not had proof of that yourself, you told me?'

'Yes. Yes, I have,' Linsie agreed softly. 'I discovered that about him when I was on the yacht.'

'Then let us have hope, hmm?' The Contessa leaned forward and waved a gloved hand. 'Here is Celik now, waiting impatiently because I am a few moments late.'

As the car slowed down at the kerb Linsie felt her heart pounding in her breast with breathless urgency, and her hands were curled tightly as they lay in her lap, sitting up close to the Contessa to make room for the additional passenger. She had hoped that he would come in from the other side and so put the Contessa between them, but there was nothing she could do about the present arrangement except get as close as she could to his mother.

At first Linsie thought he was going to refuse to join them when he saw her, for he hesitated before he got in, his head bowed, the long lean body bent double while the blue eyes swept over her as if he did not quite believe what he saw.

A second later, however, he slid on to the seat beside her and she became heart-stoppingly aware of his nearness. That familiar, tangy, spicy smell that she would always associate with him tingled in her nostrils, and the pressure of a muscular thigh against her own that was impossible to escape, like the warmth of his sleeve on her bare arm. It was all so alarmingly familiar and disturbing that she despaired of remaining cool and calm.

Briefly again, as he took his place beside her, the blue eyes swept over her face; her own eyes half concealed by the thickness of her lashes and her cheeks faintly flushed with the unexpected impact of his arrival. A faint shiver slid over her like ice water over her skin.

'We are giving Miss Palmer a ride back to her hotel, Celik,' the Contessa told him quietly, and he nodded.

'Of course,' he said coolly, as if she had been some stranger that his mother had befriended. 'I trust you are recovered, Miss Palmer.'

Linsie licked her dry lips with the tip of her tongue as the chauffeur turned the big car round and headed back the way they had come. It was just like being back at the beginning again, as if those few eventful days on the yacht had never been. Only a few short days ago she had been walking about Alanya with him, letting him buy her silk scarves and happy in his company.

He had teased her, called her Linsie, and showed concern for her when he thought she was being exposed to too much sun. Yet here he was now, sitting in close proximity to her, making her disturbingly aware of him but coolly addressing her as Miss Palmer, as if she had never become other than the hated journalist he had forcibly evicted from his estate. Perhaps, she thought despairingly, she never had been as close to him as she imagined.

'I'm—I'm much better, thank you,' she said, and

161

caught a glimpse of the Contessa's elegant brows flicking upwards in comment.

He nodded, as if he had not really been interested at all, but had simply asked out of politeness, and Linsie's heart felt cold suddenly as she faced the truth. Things were merely back to normal, as she should have expected.

As they drove back along the bright, sunny streets she tried to find words that would at least let him know how she felt about the way Kadri had behaved. Words that would in some way do something to break that cold, hurtful air of disinterest.

He said a few words to his mother in Turkish, and the Contessa shook her head, answering him in English. 'Celik,' she said, mildly scolding, 'Miss Palmer does not speak Turkish.'

'Ah!' The blue eyes were turned on her yet again, looking at her down that proud, arrogant nose. 'But you will no doubt find it convenient to learn Turkish before long, will you not, Miss Palmer?' he asked, and Linsie looked up, genuinely puzzled.

'I—I don't think so,' she denied huskily. 'I'd like to, of course, but——'

'But surely it will be necessary to some extent,' he insisted. The craggy profile was again turned against her and she watched him with the fascination of a bird with a snake, unable to take her eyes off him. 'From the manner of Kadri Lemiz,' he went on coolly, 'I assume that you are something more to him than the—brother-and-sister relationship you led me to believe, *hanim*. It will surely be to your own ad-

162

vantage and that of your future husband if you learn to speak his language—as my mother did.'

Linsie stared at him, her lips parted and her eyes blank with disbelief. 'I'm—I'm not going to marry Kadri,' she denied. Her voice was shakily husky and once more those disconcerting blue eyes were turned on her, deep and glowing, but worst of all, scornful of her denials.

'That is not the impression that Mr. Lemiz gave me when he accused me of maltreating you,' he told her harshly. 'I cannot think a man, and particularly a Turk, would behave on your behalf as he did, unless he had good grounds for doing so. I do not like being made a fool of, *hanim*, nor do I like being lied to.'

Linsie had never felt so small and unhappy in her life, and she sensed that the Contessa was in sympathy with her, even if only because of her son's violent reaction, regardless of his reasons. She felt angrily frustrated too, because it was obvious that he was in no mood to be reasoned with, and she wanted to explain about Kadri.

The thought of crying and adding to her humiliation was appalling, but the tears were already choking in her throat and her voice had a small, trembly sound. She had to be alone suddenly, anywhere away from the disturbing presence of this man who could play such havoc with her emotions, and deliver such harsh judgment on her.

'Please,' she whispered to the Contessa on her other side. 'Please will you let me out of here, Contessa?'

The Contessa looked across at her son, her eyes appealing for some sign of relenting, but there was none, and she put a gloved hand gently over Linsie's, her head shaking slowly. 'But you cannot walk so far,' she said in her soft voice. '*Mia cara bimba*, you are far from your hotel and I cannot allow you to walk, you have been unwell.'

The tears trembled on Linsie's lashes, but she bit them back determinedly. 'I can walk,' she insisted, and was already perched on the edge of her seat, her back half turned to Celik, feeling him stiff with anger behind her. 'I'll be all right, Contessa,' she said. 'Really I will, I'd rather walk.'

'Oh, but no, you——' The Contessa looked across at her son again and this time there was a note of impatience in her voice. 'Celik, you must try and persuade Miss Palmer. It is too far for her to walk after being ill.'

'Mr. Demaril isn't interested if I drop in the street!' Linsie gasped, the tears pouring down her face at last. 'I really would rather walk, please, Contessa!'

'You will sit back and ride as far as your hotel,' Celik's cool, hard voice decreed. 'It is too hot for you to walk the streets after being ill with sunstroke, and I will not be held responsible for you collapsing again.'

'I didn't say you were!' Linsie cried desperately. 'I tried to explain that you weren't responsible, and——'

164

'Your—friend believed me to be responsible,' he interrupted harshly. 'And I have no wish for you to be found unconscious in the street this time after being seen getting out of my car.'

Linsie still sat on the edge of the seat, half turned away from him, and she looked at him over her shoulder, utterly miserable and wishing she had never come out without Kadri. She had wanted so much to see Celik again, but not in circumstances like this, and certainly not to have him treat her so harshly.

'I—I wish you'd let me go,' she whispered unhappily. 'I don't want to go any further in the car, and——'

'Sit back,' he told her shortly. 'You will ride the rest of the way to your hotel and you need have no fear—my mother's presence will suffice to put your friend's mind at rest.'

Linsie said nothing; she was too stunned by the malice in his voice, puzzled too why he should be so furiously angry about Kadri. His pride surely could not still be smarting from such remarks as Kadri had had time to make about him. The Contessa would have said something more, perhaps in her defence, but he looked at her through the thickness of his dark lashes and spoke a few words in Turkish, and she subsided.

Linsie, briefly defiant and perched on the edge of the seat still, yielded at last and slid back between them, her body stiff and resentful against the unyielding warmth of him. 'Take it!'

She realised at last that a large white handkerchief

was being thrust into her hand and she took it without stopping to think, wiping the tears from her eyes and glancing up at that stern craggy profile. A gentle hand reached over and the Contessa squeezed her fingers reassuringly, her head nodding slowly, as if she was trying to convey some meaning to her.

Looking at her curiously, Linsie caught a brief glimpse of a smile in the blue eyes that were so much like her son's and she felt suddenly less unhappy, though for no good reason she could think of. She said nothing, but clenched the handkerchief she held in her hands tightly, and for a moment closed her eyes in a silent prayer.

CHAPTER TEN

'SUCH a grand arrival would be difficult to overlook,' Kadri said, and Linsie chose not to say anything in response, but to simply get on with her meal. 'And I cannot see why you see the necessity to apologise to Celik Demaril at all.' There was a glitter in his dark eyes that left Linsie in no doubt as to how angry he was. He had seen her arrive back at he hotel in the Contessa's car, but until now she had refused to discuss it with him, although it was bound to have to be discussed sooner or later, she realised.

'Why should you consider that you owe him apologies?' he insisted.

'Because you were as wrong about him as he is about you,' Linsie told him. 'I wanted him to know that the—the way you spoke to him in that *gazino* was nothing to do with me!'

Last night she had gone without her dinner rather than face his curiosity, but this morning there was little she could do about it. She sat facing him across the now familiar small table on which they had their meals and realised suddenly what a curiously intimate situation it was.

Mostly they ate alone, although sometimes there were other guests there as well, mostly Turkish people taking a break from the more scorchingly dry heat inland. Their appearance together never failed to arouse some interest, with Kadri so dark and herself so stunningly fair, but she had never been quite so aware of the seeming intimacy of their relationship until today.

Sensing an accusation in her words, Kadri looked up swiftly, his fork half way to his mouth and a small black frown between his brows. 'You are angry because I acted on your behalf?' he asked, and she shook her head.

'No, of course I'm not angry with you, Kadri, but I'm just saying that it wasn't necessary for *you* to be so angry and—carry on as you did.'

He shrugged. 'I do not understand you,' he said. 'I merely reproached the man for the way he had treated you.'

167

'But you were quite wrong about the way he treated me,' Linsie insisted. 'And flying at him the way you did, you've given him quite the wrong impression, Kadri, and he refuses to believe my explanation.'

For the moment he ignored the question of Celik's impression of him, and frowned at her again curiously. 'He was responsible for you being—unconscious,' he said. 'I had the right to be angry, and I was!'

The right to be angry. Linsie tried not to see any significance in the words, but she looked at him through the thickness of her lashes, wary of saying the wrong thing. Maybe she and Celik had misread the signs, but it was rather an unlikely coincidence for them both to have done so, and she was cautious of bringing anything into the open that could prove embarrassing to both her and Kadri.

Taking a morsel of *ciger* on to her fork, she savoured the taste of fried liver before answering him. 'You will insist that Celik was to blame for my having sunstroke,' she told him, 'and I've told you more than once, Kadri, that he wasn't.'

'He tricked you into going aboard his yacht alone,' Kadri reminded her harshly. 'That is true, Linsie, you have told me so, and I do not know what else he did to you, because you say so little about it. Such reticence makes me suspect even worse.'

'There wasn't anything worse,' she said. 'Except—well, his yacht isn't what I expected at all, he doesn't have parties on board, as I thought, and he doesn't even carry passengers. Everyone aboard is a crew member.'

It took a few seconds for the meaning of that to sink in, and when it did Kadri looked more black-browed than ever. 'I cannot believe that you were expected to become a member of his crew,' he said in a flat voice. 'I cannot believe that, Linsie.'

'Not exactly,' Linsie qualified, wishing she had not been quite so forthcoming. 'And anyway, I didn't mind in the least doing what little was expected of me—I quite liked the novelty.' She chose to ignore his look of disbelief. 'It's true I didn't know I'd be the only woman aboard,' she conceded, 'and I was very angry at first.'

'Only at first?' The dark eyes regarded her steadily, almost accusingly. 'Why did you not remain angry, Linsie?'

'Because I had no reason to!' She had not meant to sound quite so cross, but she hated being cross-examined, especially on the subject of Celik Demaril. She was much too vulnerable in that particular matter.

Kadri's good-looking face had an oddly wistful look when she looked at him again. As if he knew he would not like what he was going to hear, but must know just the same. 'He was—nice to you?' he suggested softly, and put such meaning into the simple words that Linsie flushed.

'He was nice to me,' she agreed, but refused to put any other interpretation on the words than the obvious one. 'When I was sunburned he was very kind

169

and gentle, and he even got me a scarf to cover my shoulders when we were in Alanya.'

'He deceived you about that also,' Kadri reminded her. 'It was to Side only that you were to go, he told you, instead he took you on to Alanya without my knowing, and not until you reached Alanya could you telephone me and let me know where you were.'

'That was unfortunate,' Linsie allowed, again noticing that air of possessiveness that was so new to Kadri, and which made her so uneasy.

'I had no way of knowing what had happened to you,' he said, sounding as if it was something that had been on his mind for some time. 'There was no sign of the yacht at Side, and it had not been sighted except in the distance.'

'I'm sorry, Kadri.' She looked momentarily contrite and for a moment it seemed to mollify him.

'It was not your fault,' he said. 'I know that is so, Linsie. I do not blame you.'

'But I did enjoy seeing Alanya,' she told him. 'Celik showed me around the town and treated me perfectly. I had no complaints at all.'

'Celik!' he echoed in such a way that there was no doubt how much he disliked hearing her use the name so familiarly.

'Why not?' Linsie asked quietly. 'He used my first name too. You know how I hate formality, Kadri.'

'So,' said Kadri, his dark eyes making much of the admission, 'he gave you gifts, used your first name and treated you well? Also you enjoyed yourself with him—it seems I *was* wrong about him, as you

170

claim, Linsie. I have been seeing him as your abductor, your abuser, instead he was——'

'He was kind,' Linsie interposed hastily, 'that's all, Kadri. And now he's angry because you not only misjudged him but publicly accused him as well. Not,' she added ruefully, 'that he blames you as much as he does me.'

'But how can he blame you for anything?' Kadri demanded. 'Were you not the victim, Linsie? Were you not lying there unconscious when I found you while Celik Bey sat in the *gazino* drinking coffee, even while you were trying to call me for help?'

'I *wasn't* calling for help!' She was beginning to grow really angry with him and it showed in the bright sparkle of her eyes as she looked at him. 'You had no cause to speak to him as you did, Kadri, and you gave him quite the wrong impression—that's why he blames me, because he thinks I deliberately lied to him about you!'

'I do not understand.'

Linsie did not altogether believe him, and she sighed as she tried to explain. 'I told Celik that you were acting on your father's behalf in caring for me,' she told him. 'I told him how your family had—well, adopted me while I'm staying in Turkey, and I said you were like a brother to me.'

'I see.'

He did not look up and she pressed on hastily. 'When you made so much fuss about my fainting and you were so—so angry and rude to him, he thought you had—more than brotherly reasons for

171

behaving as you did.'

Kadri was not looking at her but down at his plate, and he seemed to have completely lost interest in his meal, pushing it around his plate with the fork. 'Is that also why you are so angry, Linsie?' he asked quietly, and she stared at him for a moment, then licked her lips nervously.

'I—I don't quite know what to make of you lately,' she confessed. 'I've tried to convince Celik that you were simply worried about me as a good friend would be, but——' She shrugged uneasily, looking across at him through her lashes, a strange sense of sadness making her wish she had never brought matters this far. 'He—he won't believe me,' she said huskily.

'And it is important to you that he believes you?' Kadri asked.

Linsie nodded, recognising it as the truth. It mattered a great deal to her that Celik believed there was nothing more between her and Kadri than close friendship, although it was doubtful if he would care one way or the other—despite that encouraging gesture of the Contessa's yesterday.

'Yes,' she admitted after a moment, 'it's important to me, Kadri.'

The dark eyes lifted at last and she met their bright, glowing gaze head on. 'I was afraid it would be so,' he said softly.

'Kadri——' She reached out and touched his hand, her fingertips gentle and seeking to reassure or console, she was uncertain which at the moment.

'You can perhaps guess how it is I feel for you,

Linsie,' he said in a soft, quiet voice that touched her heart dangerously.

For a moment she said nothing, unable to find the right words, looking down at her own hand as it clasped his, and feeling rather as if she had in some odd way, let him down. Until the past few days she had had no inkling that Kadri felt anything more for her than friendship. A close friendship, it was true, but nothing more, and discovering that he loved her made her feel guilty in some strange way.

'I— I didn't know,' she whispered.

It entered her head at that moment that perhaps she ought to draw back her hand because Selim Bey was looking in their direction and he might possibly put his own construction on that small, intimate gesture. Kadri, however, seemed unaware of anyone else but themselves in the room, and he still held her gaze steadily.

'I thought you knew it,' he said softly. 'I love you, Linsie, and until recently I thought—I hoped you felt something for me too.' The dark eyes had a luminous, soulful look that could so easily have been her undoing had it not been for other, blue, eyes so firmly fixed in her mind's eye.

'Oh, Kadri!'

Never in her life before had she been called upon to face such a situation and she felt horribly vulnerable and helpless. She hated so much having to hurt Kadri, but there was nothing she could do but let him know the truth before he misunderstood her again. It was almost as if she had lost them both

173

suddenly. Celik she would almost certainly never see again, and Kadri would never be able to look at her in the same tolerantly friendly way he had until now.

'Do not look so sad,' he said softly, and smiled as he turned his hand to enfold hers. 'I did not truly expect you to love me, Linsie, however much I hoped I was wrong.' He flicked his dark gaze in the direction of the hovering Selim Bey and shook his head. 'Now we will finish our meal and give Selim Bey no more cause for speculation,' he told her with an attempt at lightness. 'Eat your *ciger* and try not to look so unhappy, or Selim will surely think I am being unkind to you!'

Linsie felt a hazy, moist sensation in her eyes as she too glanced across at Selim Bey, then back again at Kadri. 'I seem to have learned so much while I've been here,' she said in a small, wistful voice, as she picked up her fork again. 'Somehow I seem to have become so much—older.'

Kadri smiled at her across the little table, shaking his head, his eyes glowing darkly. 'You still look like a golden-haired little girl,' he told her softly. 'And unless he is a man made of ice, which I cannot believe of any countryman of mine, Celik Demaril will find you as hard to forget as I would, my Linsie.'

There was no real reason why they should stay on in Antalya, Linsie realised, but Kadri had not so far suggested that they leave, and she was very reluctant to do so until she was obliged to.

She had ample material to write quite an illuminating feature about Celik Demaril, even though Kadri

174

had managed to obtain no pictures of him, but there was more involved now than the writing of an article about him.

Kadri had spoken of it as fact, but Linsie herself still hesitated to face the fact that she was in love with Celik, too hopelessly in love with him to simply pack up and leave Antalya without even trying to see him again.

Looked at in the cold light of common sense, it seemed a hopeless cause, but like any woman in love, Linsie refused to believe her dream had no chance of coming true. She had cabled her father that she would be coming home some time, but that she was enjoying herself too much at the moment to even think about it. Such liberties with the truth were permissible, she thought, in the circumstances.

It was one morning when she was actually beginning to see her prolonged stay as nothing but a waste of time and money that Selim Bey announced a telephone call for her. He made great show of calling her to the telephone, then smiled all over his wide brown face and indicated the instrument with a hint of a bow.

'The Contessa Contini, *hanim*,' he told her. 'Very private, I understand.'

Linsie nodded, unable to find her voice for a second, then she took up the instrument with hands that shook, and spoke her name into it. 'Miss Palmer?' The Contessa sounded even more soft-voiced over the telephone. 'Ah, good!'

'Good morning, Contessa!' She tried to keep her

175

voice steady, but there was a betraying huskiness in it that she hoped would not be noticed.

'I wished to learn how you were,' the Contessa told her. 'It is several days since I saw you, Miss Palmer, and you were—somewhat distraught then, I was afraid you might be unwell again.'

'Oh no, no, I'm fine, thank you, Contessa!' She could not help suspecting that there was some other reason behind the call than a desire to learn how she was, and Linsie sought for reasons as she listened.

'Ah, I am so glad! I wondered if perhaps——' The hesitation was significant in itself, and it had Linsie's pulses racing wildly. 'I thought perhaps you would care to visit me one day,' the Contessa went on in her soft, gentle voice, and gave a light laugh. 'I shall be alone in a few days' time, you see, and I like company —my reasons are purely selfish, you see, Miss Palmer!'

Linsie did not for one minute believe it, but she went along with the charade for the moment, wondering what exactly was expected of her. 'Alone?' she echoed, and the Contessa laughed again.

'I am afraid so,' she said. 'My son has decided to desert me, Miss Palmer. He is flying to Rome in two days' time, on some mad impulse that he seems to have no reason for, but——' Linsie could imagine those slim, elegant shoulders shrugging carelessly. 'What can I do about it?'

Her heart was beating so hard she could scarcely breathe and there was a coldness in her that resisted even the heat of the tiny kiosk. If Celik was going away it would be the end of her hopes, there would never be another chance for her.

'Contessa——' She hesitated, her heart urging her on, her natural reticence holding her back. But it was the more urgent need that won eventually and she licked her lips hastily before she went on. 'I—I might be going back myself in a few days' time,' she said. 'If—perhaps if I could come soon, perhaps——'

'This afternoon?' the Contessa suggested softly. 'That will be ideal, Miss Palmer.'

'You're sure it isn't—inconvenient?' Linsie asked anxiously, already seeing her impulsive action as just the sort of thing that Celik Demaril would frown upon. He had made it clear more than once that he disliked a woman to take the initiative.

'It will be ideal,' the Contessa assured her, and paused briefly. 'I promise you that it will not prove an—embarrassing visit, *mia cara bimba*,' she added softly. 'Please come, for all our sakes, hmm?'

The invitation was irresistible, although deep down Linsie had many doubts and her legs already felt weaker than water as she stood beside the telephone. 'I'll come, Contessa,' she said huskily. 'And—thank you.'

It was difficult telling Kadri where she was going, and when she eventually did break it to him it was obvious how he felt about the visit from his worried frown. 'Oh, Linsie, how can you be sure?' he asked. His dark eyes searched her face for a moment, anxious and unhappy. 'You will do much to see him again, will you not?' he asked softly, and she nodded without hesitation.

'I can't just let him fly out of my life, Kadri,' she said, her eyes anxiously seeking his approval. 'I know how it must look, especially to a man like you or like —like Celik, but I have to try, one last time, to see him.'

Kadri looked down at her for a moment, then he nodded, as if he understood. 'And you wish me to drive you there?' he asked.

Linsie nodded. 'I know you wanted the car this afternoon,' she said. 'But I'd rather you drove me than I had a taxi up there, Kadri.' She smiled ruefully as she faced the possibility of actually being turned away. 'If he—if he won't let me in, then I can always walk down again, like I did once before,' she told him.

Kadri's dark eyes searched the pale soft oval of her face for a few seconds, then he smiled and shook his head. 'He will not turn you away,' he told her softly. 'It is not possible.'

'Then you'll take me?'

Again he nodded. 'I will take you,' he said.

The hill road had not seemed so long before, and Linsie had no eyes for the magnificent scenery this time, but looked straight ahead, her hands clasped tightly in her lap as Kadri drove at his customary breakneck speed. She did not even notice or remark on his driving this time, but sat wrapped in her own thoughts, reliving the last time they had driven up here.

Farik, the house in the hills, was already visible through the lush greenery of its surroundings, and she felt her heart give a violent lurch when she caught sight of it for the first time. The Contessa had invited her, ostensibly as her guest, but it was all too evident what her main purpose was, and for the first time Linsie wondered at her apparent readiness to act as peacemaker.

With a son as attractive and wealthy as Celik Demaril she surely had many opportunities to matchmake, and it was all the more surprising to find her ready to act as she was for the the sake of a young foreign journalist, some years her son's junior.

'You are nervous?' She turned her head, startled by Kadri speaking, and then nodded.

'A little,' she confessed. 'But we're nearly there now.'

The impressive gates of Farik loomed before them, as they had on that first occasion, and Linsie's heart began a wild and uncontrollable tattoo against her ribs. Kadri braked the little car to a halt and turned to look at her, his eyes still anxious.

'Shall I wait?' he asked, but she shook her head.

'No,' she said. 'I'll be all right, Kadri, thank you.'

He was not happy, she knew that, and he would have waited no matter what other business he had down in the town, but she waved a hand at him as she got out of the car and walked across to those imposing gates, her fair hair lifted and blown by the same warm wind from the sea.

She had no hat on, because she did not anticipate

being very long in the sun, and a new dress of soft blue silk brushed softly against her legs as she walked. She heard the car reverse and drive off back down the hill with Kadri's voice lingering vaguely in her ears, but she was concerned with being expected by that same short, stocky little man who guarded the gates.

There appeared to be no one about at the moment and she felt the first tremble of doubt in her stomach as she looked through those forbidding bars at the lush garden beyond. No one was there, even the trees and shrubs that crowded the garden with scent and colour seemed still, despite that warm soft wind.

Then she saw him. Not the little guardian of the gates but Celik Demaril himself and looking so much as she had first seen him that she could almost believe she had gone back in time.

A cream-coloured suit tailored to fit that lean, sinewy body to perfection and a brown shirt, open at the neck and exposing the length of his throat. He came on long, smooth strides and there was no clue in his expression as to what his mood might be, so that Linsie watched him anxiously.

He did not look at her until he stood immediately the other side of the gate from her, then the blue eyes looked at her steadily, bringing a faint flush to her cheeks and a wildly uncontrollable beat to her heart. 'You have not walked?' he asked as he opened the gates with the same key he took from his pocket when he had evicted her so forcibly before.

Linsie shook her head, her legs trembling and as

weak as water as she stood before him, acutely conscious of that disturbing aura of masculinity surrounding him. That same tangy, spicy smell that she always would associate with him even if he did send her away again.

'Kadri brought me,' she said in a small, husky voice, and one dark brow flicked swiftly upwards.

'And left you?' he asked softly.

Linsie raised her eyes and met his with far more confidence than she was feeling. 'He has somewhere else to go,' she told him. 'I didn't anticipate being ordered away on this occasion since the Contessa invited me.'

She sounded much more bold than she had meant to, but she was almost sure he saw through it, and a small hint of smile gave her the clue. The blue eyes studied her for a moment longer, then he took her arm and the unexpected gesture almost had her starting visibly.

The touch of those strong brown fingers on her skin evoked sensations she could not control, and the warmth of his body touched her each time she took a step. 'My mother is like most women,' he said quietly. 'Devious and quite capable of getting her own way without appearing to do so.'

'I—I don't know——' Linsie began, but he laughed and looked down at her, his blue eyes bright and glittering as if he was enjoying the situation.

'I do,' he told her. 'By inviting you here, she is hoping to achieve something she has so far failed to do.'

181

Linsie licked her lips, no longer sure that she knew what any of it was about. She was content at the moment to be doing no more than walking through these beautiful gardens with his hand under her arm and the warm, exciting nearness of him playing havoc with her senses.

'I don't know what the Contessa wants to see me for,' she ventured, but as before she was cut short by a short but not altogether humourless laugh.

'Don't you?' he asked softly.

They were standing on the same curving path that ran round from the back of the house, under the shadow of the flowering shrubs, their scent full and heady in the sun. It was almost the exact spot where he had captured her so dramatically the last time she came to Farik.

A huge magnolia, backed by roses and the dark slim beauty of cypress, shaded them from the heat and Linsie had not the strength or the inclination to resist the hand that held her there. There was no one else about and the scent of the magnolia was like incense, its waxy blossoms just stirring in the warm wind off the sea.

'Mr. Demaril——'

'Celik,' he interrupted softly. 'Must we be so formal?'

It took her a moment to recognise her own words and then she barely resisted a smile. 'I—I don't want you to get the wrong idea about—about why I'm here,' she said in a small and very unsteady voice.

'I don't think I have.' She looked up at him, frankly

puzzled. The blue eyes were brighter than she had ever seen them and every nerve in her body cried out for him, but she had to be much more sure. 'I know why my mother asked you to visit her,' he told her quietly. 'I also know that you came just as quickly as you could, Linsie Hanim.'

'Mr. Demaril——'

'Celik!'

'Celik! Oh, please, I don't know why you're doing this, but I know you must be—be trying to put me in my place again and I don't—I can't——'

'Linsie! Linsie, listen to me!'

He shook her gently and she stared up at him with wide, unbelieving eyes, her heart racing like a mad thing in her breast. 'You can't mean to be—nice to me,' she whispered. 'I know you can't, not after the other day when you said all those cruel things, when you treated me as if I was a—a liar and a cheat!'

'I believed you were,' he said quietly. 'I was angry because you had made a fool of me, and I am not a very forgiving man, Linsie.'

'I *didn't* make a fool of you!'

The wide mouth curled into a wry smile, a smile that was reflected in his blue eyes as he looked down at her. 'So my mother has convinced me,' he told her dryly. 'Though I am not at all sure that I do not believe her simply because I *want* to believe her.'

'Celik——' She shook her head. 'I wish I knew what it was all about.'

For a moment he said nothing, then he smiled slowly, a smile that set her pulses whirling again.

183

'Kadri Lemiz is a sad young man, I think,' he said softly. 'I was not wrong when I said he was in love with you, Linsie, was I?'

She shook her head, frowning at the memory of Kadri's touching declaration. 'No,' she whispered. 'You weren't.'

'But you didn't realise it?' Again she shook her head. 'As you did not realise that I was falling in love with you,' he added softly.

She looked up swiftly, catching a warmth in those blue eyes that did strange and exciting things to her emotions. 'I—I don't know,' she whispered.

'Oh, Linsie,' he said softly, 'are you really such a blind little creature?'

Linsie looked up at him for one breathless moment, her eyes searching that strong, craggy face for reassurance that he meant what he was saying, that he was not simply acting out some vengeful fantasy of his own.

'All her married life my mother has dreamed of my marrying a golden-haired, blue-eyed girl,' he said, his own blue eyes glowing warmly. 'She could not believe it when she found me chasing you from my garden that day. You were just like her own youthful image, when she married my father. I think I too knew even then that I was going to find you much too hard to forget, despite the way you angered me with your persistence.'

The sudden warm pressure of his arms about her set her senses reeling again and she hesitated only briefly before sliding her hands up round his neck.

184

'I was more than willing to be convinced that you had not made a fool of me about Kadri,' he said. 'I had made plans to fly to Rome in a day or so, but when Mama said that you would be coming——' He shrugged his broad shoulders and smiled wryly down at her. 'I wanted to believe you were coming to see me and not Mama.'

'I did,' Linsie said softly. 'I was so—so miserable that I was about to pack up and go home, and then the Contessa rang and said that you were going away and——'

'And you came to me,' he said softly. 'You came to try and change my mind, to make me see what I would be losing if I went away and let you go out of my life.'

She looked up at him, eyes wide and bright, pressed close to the warm strength of him. 'You believe me now?' she asked, and he smiled, his hands pulling her closer to him.

'I believe you,' he said softly.

The last time he had kissed her it had been in anger, so she had believed, but there was no anger this time, only a fierce but gentle pressure she could not resist. At first he did no more than just lightly touch her mouth, then his lips parted hers and he took her mouth fiercely, hungrily, like a man in desperate need.

Strong hands moulded her softness to the sinewy strength of his body and she clung to him, thrillingly aware of the needs of her own body for the first time, her hands holding tightly to the thick brown hair at the back of his neck, her mouth responding willingly with an abandon she would never have believed herself capable of.

When he raised his head at last, she buried her own against the broadness of his chest and breathed deeply of that spicy tang, her hands tightly curled against his chest. The gently smoothing touch of a hand over her fair hair made her stir in his arms, and he put a hand under her chin to raise her face to him.

'I shall make you wear the veil,' he said in a deep, quiet voice. 'I will never have peace of mind otherwise, for fear there are more Kadris waiting to take you away from me.'

Linsie shook her head, her eyes bright and shining as she looked up at that beloved dark face, she had thought she would never see again. Her sudden exultant laughter tipped back her head and he buried his face in the golden softness of her hair, his mouth pressed to the small, throbbing pulse at the base of her throat.

'We will sail around the world for ever,' he murmured, 'so that I shall have you to myself always.'

Linsie looked across to where the tall iron gates stood like guardians at the end of the garden, the big key still in the lock, and she smiled. 'We could stay here,' she suggested with a smile. 'I never again want to be on the outside of those gates, shut off from you, my darling.'

Celik, gathering her to him, walked back to the

gates and turned the key in the lock. Removing it and handing it to her, he smiled. 'You shall hold the key to the gate, my love, you already have the key to my heart.'

Mills & Boon
Best Seller Romances

The very best of Mills & Boon
brought back for those of you
who missed reading them when they
were first published.
There are three other Best Seller Romances
for you to collect this month.

DARLING JENNY
by Janet Dailey

Jennifer Glenn, smarting from a disastrous love affair, had
taken herself off to the skiing grounds of Wyoming to 'get
away from it all' and lend a hand to her busy sister Sheila at
the same time. She never expected to fall in love again so
soon, and certainly not with the man who was himself in
love with Sheila!

THE MAN AT KAMBALA
by Kay Thorpe

Sara lived with her father at Kambala in Kenya and was
accustomed to do as she pleased there. She certainly didn't
think much of Steve York, the impossible man who came to
take charge in her father's absence. 'It's asking for trouble to
run around a game reserve as if it were a play park,' he told
her. Was Sara right to ignore him?

FOOD FOR LOVE
by Rachel Lindsay

Amanda could see problems ahead when her boss, Clive Brand,
began taking serious interest in her, so she changed her job.
And found still more problems in the person of that mysterious
maddening man, Red Clark!

**If you have difficulty in obtaining any of these books through
your local paperback retailer, write to:**

Mills & Boon Reader Service
P.O. Box 236, Thornton Road, Croydon, Surrey, CR9 3RU.

Doctor Nurse Romances

and April's
stories of romantic relationships behind the scenes
of modern medical life are:

CHILDREN'S NURSE
by Kathryn Blair

Nurse Linda Grey travels to Portugal to look after
four-year old Jacinto but her modern ideas meet with
strong opposition from the boy's father, the handsome
Marquez de Filano.

MAJOR MIKE
by Hazel Fisher

When under Major Mike's command at the Territorial
Army camp, Nurse Lisa Hilton tries hard to ignore his
sarcastic comments, only to find she is haunted by
the Major's piercing dark eyes . . .

The Mills & Boon Rose is the Rose of Romance

Every month there are ten new titles to choose from — ten new stories about people falling in love, people you want to read about, people in exciting, far-away places. Choose Mills & Boon. It's your way of relaxing:

April's titles are:

THE STORM EAGLE by *Lucy Gillen*
In other circumstances Chiara would have married Campbell Roberts. But he had not consulted her. And now wild horses wouldn't make her accept him!

SECOND-BEST BRIDE by *Margaret Rome*
Angie would never have guessed how the tragedy that had befallen Terzan Helios would affect her own life . . .

WOLF AT THE DOOR by *Victoria Gordon*
Someone had to win the battle of wills betwwen Kelly Barnes and her boss Grey Scofield, in their Rocky Mountains camp . . .

THE LIGHT WITHIN by *Yvonne Whittal*
Now that Roxy might recover her sight, the misunderstanding between her and the Marcus Fleming seemed too great for anything to bridge it . . .

SHADOW DANCE by *Margaret Way*
If only her new job assignment had helped Alix to sort out the troubled situation between herself and her boss Carl Danning!

SO LONG A WINTER by *Jane Donnelly*
'You'll always be too young and I'll always be too old,' Matt Hanlon had told Angela five years ago. Was the situation any different now?

NOT ONCE BUT TWICE by *Betty Neels*
Christina had fallen in love at first sight with Professor Adam ter Brandt. But hadn't she overestimated his interest in her?

MASTER OF SHADOWS by *Susanna Firth*
The drama critic Max Anderson had wrecked Vanessa's acting career with one vicious notice, and then Vanessa became his secretary . . .

THE TRAVELLING KIND by *Janet Dailey*
Charley Collins knew that she must not get emotionally involved with Shad Russell. But that was easier said than done . . .

ZULU MOON by *Gwen Westwood*
In order to recover from a traumatic experience Julie went to Zululand, and once again fell in love with a man who was committed elsewhere . . .

If you have difficulty in obtaining any of these books from your local paperback retailer, write to:

Mills & Boon Reader Service
P.O. Box 236, Thornton Road, Croydon, Surrey, CR9 3RU.

Masquerade
Historical Romances

Intrigue excitement romance

THE RELUCTANT MATCH
by Polly Meyrick

Sophie modelled her conduct on that of the heroines
of her favourite novels. But not even Lenore, in *The
Prisoner of the Vampire,* was ordered to marry an old,
balding stranger! So Sophie ran away to London and
met the mysterious Mr Fanshawe, who looked like a
hero and behaved like a villain ...

GLEN OF FROST
by Belinda Grey

Fiona Seidhe Maclaren was caught in a bitter struggle
when she fell in love with her cousin Lachlan. Forced
to marry his bastard brother, Jamie, she became the
prize in a blood feud that reached its climax at the
Battle of Culloden, where brother fought brother.
Could her love survive such bitter hatred?

**Look out for these titles in your local paperback shop from
10th April 1981**

Mills & Boon
Best Seller Romances

The very best of Mills & Boon Romances
brought back for those of you who missed
them when they were first published.

In May
we bring back the following four
great romantic titles.

COUNTRY OF THE FALCON
by Anne Mather

When Alexandra went to the uncivilised regions of the Amazon
to look for her father she was prepared to find life different
from the security of her English home. She certainly didn't
expect, however, to find herself at the mercy of the devastatingly
attractive Declan O'Rourke and to be forced to accompany him
to his mountain retreat at Paradiablo.

FORBIDDEN RAPTURE
by Violet Winspear

When Della Neve went on a Mediterranean cruise, she wasn't
looking for a holiday romance. Her future was already bound to
Marsh Graham, the fiance to whom she owed everything. But on
board ship she encountered Nicholas di Fioro Franquila, who
treated women as playthings. Was Della an exception?

THE BENEDICT MAN
by Mary Wibberley

Lovely surroundings and a kind and considerate employer —
Beth was delighted at the prospect of her new job in Derbyshire.
But when she arrived at Benedict House she discovered that it
was not the sympathetic Mrs. Thornburn who required her
services as a secretary, but her arrogant and completely unreasonable nephew. Could Beth put up with his insufferable attitude
towards her?

TILL THE END OF TIME
by Lilian Peake

As far as Marisa was concerned Dirk was no longer part of her
life. So it came as a great shock to her when he returned, even
more dictatorial and exasperating than she remembered him,
to disrupt her calm again. Of course, it wasn't as if he meant
anything to her now. Yet why did she find herself wondering
about his relationship with the glamorous Luella?

**If you have difficulty in obtaining any of these books through
your local paperback retailer, write to:**

Mills & Boon Reader Service
P.O. Box 236, Thornton Road, Croydon, Surrey, CR9 3RU.